Teggs is no ordinary dinosaur –
he's an **ASTROSAUR!** Captain of
the amazing spaceship DSS *Sauropod*,
he goes on dangerous missions and
fights evil – along with his faithful
crew, Gipsy, Arx and Iggy.

Join them now in this special,
extra-long adventure!

For more astro-fun visit the website
www.astrosaurs.co.uk

*Read all the adventures of*
*Teggs, Gipsy, Arx and Iggy!*

*Read the full set of Astrosaurs Academy adventures!*

Find out more at www.astrosaurs.co.uk

# Astrosaurs

## EARTH ATTACK!

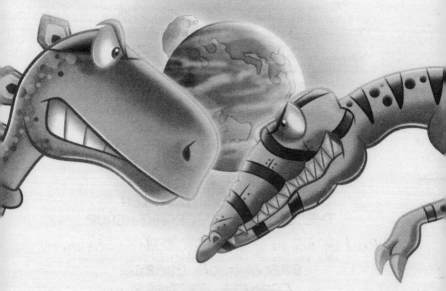

Steve Cole

*Illustrated by* Woody Fox

**RED FOX**

**EARTH ATTACK**
**A RED FOX BOOK 978 1 849 41899 7**

First published in Great Britain by Red Fox,
an imprint of Random House Children's Publishers UK
A Random House Group Company

This edition published 2012

The Random House Group Limited supports The Forest Stewardship Council (FSC®), the
leading international forest certification organisation. Our books carrying the FSC label are
printed on FSC® certified paper. FSC is the only forest certification scheme endorsed by the
leading environmental organisations, including Greenpeace. Our paper procurement
policy can be found at www.randomhouse.co.uk/environment

MIX
Paper from
responsible sources
FSC® C016897

Red Fox Books are published by Random House Children's Publishers UK,
61–63 Uxbridge Road, London W5 5SA

www.**randomhousechildrens**.co.uk
www.**totallyrandombooks**.co.uk

Addresses for companies within The Random House Group Limited can
be found at: www.randomhouse.co.uk/offices.htm

THE RANDOM HOUSE GROUP Limited Reg. No. 954009

A CIP catalogue record for this book is available from the British Library.

Printed and bound in Great Britain by CPI Group (UK) Ltd,
Croydon, CR0 4YY

*For Beau, Ashton and Alfie Clifford*

# WARNING!

## THINK YOU KNOW ABOUT DINOSAURS?

### THINK AGAIN!

The dinosaurs ...

Big, stupid, lumbering reptiles. Right?

All they did was eat, sleep and roar a bit. Right?

Died out millions of years ago when a big meteor struck the Earth. Right?

*Wrong!*

The dinosaurs weren't stupid. They may have had small brains, but they used them well. They had big thoughts and big dreams.

By the time the meteor hit, the last dinosaurs had already left Earth for ever. Some breeds had discovered how to travel through space as early as the Triassic period, and were already enjoying a new life among the stars. No one has found evidence of dinosaur technology yet. But the first fossil bones were only unearthed in 1822, and new finds are being made all the time.

The proof is out there, buried in the ground.

And the dinosaurs live on, way out in space, even now. They've settled down in a place they call the Jurassic Quadrant and over the last sixty-five million years they've gone on evolving.

The dinosaurs we'll be meeting are

 part of a special group called the Dinosaur Space Service. Their job is to explore space, to go on exciting missions and to fight evil and protect the innocent!

These heroic herbivores are not just dinosaurs.

They are *astrosaurs*!

*NOTE: The following story has been translated from secret Dinosaur Space Service records. Earthling dinosaur names are used throughout, although some changes have been made for easy reading. There's even a guide to help you pronounce the dinosaur names on the next page.*

# Talking Dinosaur!

How to say the prehistoric names
in this book . . .

STEGOSAURUS –
*STEG-oh-SORE-us*

CARNOTAUR –
*kar-noh-TOR*

IGUANODON –
*ig-WA-noh-don*

DIPLODOCUS –
*di-PLOH-de-kus*

HADROSAUR –
*HAD-roh-sore*

OVIRAPTOR –
*OH-vee-RAP-tor*

TRICERATOPS –
*try-SERRA-tops*

MEGALOSAURUS –
*MEG-ah-loh-SORE-us*

BAROSAURUS –
*bar-oh-SORE-us*

SPINOSAURUS –
*SPY-nuh-SORE-us*

CRYPTOCLIDUS –
*crip-toh-CLYD-us*

ALLOSAURUS –
*AL-uh-SORE-us*

VELOCIRAPTOR –
*vel-ossi-RAP-tor*

BARYONYX –
*bare-ee-ON-iks*

DIMORPHODON –
*die-MORF-oh-don*

PLATEOSAURUS –
*PLAY-tee-a-SORE-us*

PTEROSAUR –
*TEH-roh-sore*

PTERODACTYL –
*teh-roh-DACT-il*

# THE CREW OF THE DSS SAUROPOD

**CAPTAIN
TEGGS STEGOSAUR**

**ARX ORANO,**
FIRST OFFICER

**GIPSY SAURINE,**
COMMUNICATIONS
OFFICER

**IGGY TOOTH,**
CHIEF ENGINEER

# Jurassic Quadrant

Ankylos

Steggos

Diplox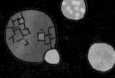

INDEPENDENT
DINOSAUR
ALLIANCE

vegetarian
sector

Squawk
Major

DSS
UNION OF
PLANETS

PTEROSAURIA

Tri System    Corytho    Lambeos

Iguanos

Aqua Minor

Geldos Cluster

Teerex Major

Olympus

TYRANNOSAUR
TERRITORIES

anet Sixty

carnivore
sector

Raptos

THEROPOD EMPIRE

Megalos

Cryptos

vegmeat
zone
(neutral space)

EA REPTILE
SPACE

Pliosaur
Nurseries

Not to scale

# EARTH ATTACK!

# Chapter One

## TIME FOR DANGER

"The waiting's over!" cried Teggs Stegosaur, bursting into the metal meeting room. "I've just seen Admiral Rosso in the corridor. He's on his way here right now!"

Teggs was captain of the DSS *Sauropod* – the fastest ship in the Dinosaur Space Service. He had flown, fought and hungrily munched his way through countless galactic adventures, helped always by his

1

brilliant crewmates Arx, Iggy and Gipsy.
They were sitting inside the *Sauropod*'s
meeting room, and looked as excited as
he was.

"Rosso's in charge of the whole DSS,"
remarked Iggy, the gruff iguanodon
engineer. "Whatever he wants, it must be
something big."

"I bet he's going to give us a super-
top-secret mission," said Gipsy, the
stripy hadrosaur in charge of the ship's
communications. "Something only we
can handle."

Arx, Teggs's brainy triceratops deputy,
smiled. "Let's hope we *can* handle it –
whatever it is."

The sound of heavy footsteps carried from outside. "We'll soon find out," said Teggs, quickly taking his seat at the head of the meeting table. "Here he comes!"

Admiral Rosso, a long-necked brown barosaurus, pushed inside and peered down at Teggs and his crew through his glasses. "Ah, hello, astrosaurs." He beamed. "Guess what? You're all going to space prison!"

Teggs gulped. "Er . . . have we done something wrong, sir?"

"Yeah, normally we put bad guys behind bars," said Iggy. "We don't go there ourselves!"

But Arx just smiled. "I think Admiral Rosso means he wants us to *visit* a space prison."

3

"Your clever first officer is quite correct, Teggs," said Rosso. "Have you ever heard of a sea-reptile called Zindi Bent?"

"I remember her from the space news," said Gipsy. "She was an inventor, wasn't she?"

Arx nodded. "She invented automatic robbing machines for that bunch of sea-reptile criminals, the Doom-Flipper Squad."

"That's what we believed," Rosso agreed. "The DSS arrested her five years ago. But she has always insisted the Doom-Flipper Squad stole her designs for automatic mining robots and changed them to make machines that suited their own evil ends."

"But she couldn't prove it," Gipsy recalled.

"Which is why she wound up in space prison," said Rosso. "But Prison Governor Bunwinkle has always believed Zindi was innocent. And since her capture, under his watchful eye, she has spent most of her time in the secure workshop, stretching her inventive powers to the limit, trying to create the only thing that can prove her innocence . . . a time machine!"

The astrosaurs stared at Rosso in amazement.

"It sounds incredible, I know. But Bunwinkle assures me she has succeeded." Rosso pressed a button on the meeting table and a TV screen slid up from the smooth surface. He slid a video-disk into its side. "Take a look at this."

Teggs watched as a smart but waterlogged study appeared on the screen. Moments later two nasty-looking yellow cryptoclidus slithered in through the study window and set about a safe with their flippers.

Arx jumped up in his seat. "But . . . they're the ringleaders of the Doom-Flipper Gang!"

"And that is Zindi's study," Rosso informed him, as the robbers on the screen broke open the safe and stole the papers inside.

"Sure enough, they are stealing her designs."

"Then this is the proof that she was telling the truth," said Gipsy. "Why didn't she show anyone sooner?"

"Because this video was taken only a few days ago – by *Governor Bunwinkle himself*!" Rosso turned off the TV with an excited flourish. "Bunwinkle test-drove her machine. He travelled back five years into the past and recorded those slippery villains in the act."

Arx's horns waggled in astonishment. "Then . . . her time machine really works?"

"Come off it!" Iggy spluttered. "I bet that scene was staged somehow. It's all a trick!"

"Perhaps," said Rosso. "That is why I am going to examine Zindi's work for myself."

"It could be the most amazing invention in history," said Arx.

Teggs nodded. "Or the most dangerous."

"A time machine would indeed be a terrible weapon in the wrong hands," Rosso agreed. "That's why I want my finest astrosaurs to guard it — and why I came here to see you instead of telling you over a communicator. I couldn't risk the message being overheard by carnivore spies."

"I'll give the order to increase the ship's speed." Teggs jumped from his seat and ran out of the meeting room. "The sooner we arrive, the better!"

Within the hour, the space prison was looming large through the *Sauropod*'s

portholes. It was a massive castle of
rusting metal, crammed full of carnivore
crooks. As the egg-shaped ship touched
down in the landing bay, Teggs felt an
uneasy prickle travel along his spiky tail.

"I don't see why a time machine is so
dangerous," said Gipsy, joining Teggs,
Iggy and Arx as they walked with Rosso
to the exit.

"If you mess about in the past, you
could end up affecting the future," said
Arx. "Just imagine if Iggy travelled back
to the year his brother hatched and then
accidentally stepped on that egg . . ."

Iggy gulped. "Wimvis would never have been born!"

"And his life would never have happened," Teggs agreed. "You'd have changed history – and not in a good way."

He opened the *Sauropod*'s doors and Rosso led the way outside.

"Aha! There you are." A large and somewhat lumpy grey diplodocus in a white suit waved from the inner door. "I'm Bunwinkle, the governor here."

"Yes, of course." Rosso smiled. "We spoke over the communicator. Funny, you sound different in the flesh."

"I've got a cold," said Bunwinkle, and he sniffed noisily to prove it.

"Did you really travel back through time?" Gipsy asked eagerly.

Bunwinkle looked surprised. "Eh?"

"You took a video camera and recorded the Doom-Flipper Squad," Arx reminded him.

"That bunch of amateurs!" Bunwinkle snarled. "Well, the thing is, I think Zindi Bent was tricking me. I want you astrosaurs to test her machine for yourselves. I've got her chained up in the crew room, ready to begin her demonstration."

"Chained up?" Teggs frowned. "I thought you just proved she was innocent?"

"Look, do you want to test this time machine or don't you?" said Bunwinkle, wobbling off along the bare metal corridor. "Follow me."

"Are you OK?" asked Gipsy. "You look a bit unsteady on your feet."

"I'm fine." Bunwinkle glowered at them.

11

"I just banged my head this morning . . . on an inmate's nose. Now, keep up!"

"He seems very mean," muttered Gipsy.

"I suppose in a place full of crooks, you have to be," Iggy whispered back.

Suddenly a stegosaurus in a strange helmet and a shirt covered with gold discs burst out through a doorway in front of them. The astrosaurs stared in stunned amazement.

And none stared closer than Captain Teggs . . .

Incredibly – impossibly – the stegosaurus was an identical version of himself!

## Chapter Two

## THE TIME TEST

"It works!" cried the second Teggs, grinning at his astounded audience. "It actually works!"

"Who are you?" the real Teggs demanded.

But the newcomer ducked back through the door and slammed it behind him.

"Wait!" The real Teggs pushed past Bunwinkle and threw open the door to reveal a long corridor – which was empty. The single door at its far end was shut. "That stegosaurus was a perfect double of me! Where'd he go?"

"Whoever he was, he must be wearing a costume to make himself look like you," Iggy declared.

"Eh? A costume to make him look like someone else?" Bunwinkle rounded on Iggy. "Don't be ridiculous! That could never happen!"

"Then how do you explain Teggs being in two places at once, Bunwinkle?" asked Rosso sternly. "Could your inmates be playing a trick?"

"Your double even *sounded* like you, Captain," said Gipsy.

"I think we should ask Zindi Bent about it." Bunwinkle stomped off on his wobbly legs into the corridor. "Now!"

Teggs and his friends followed the limping governor to the

door at the end. A
strange whirring,
rustling sound
came from within.
Bunwinkle threw
open the door onto
a large, well-lit
room filled with
games and chairs
and TVs. Usually
the prison warders
relaxed here, but
right now there was

just one small sea-reptile inside, her back
turned to them, her body weighed down
with chains. She was sitting fuming
beside a small pyramid-shaped machine
that was covered in switches, screens and
levers.

"So that's Zindi Bent," Arx murmured,
"and that must be her time machine."

"Governor Bunwinkle," said the sea-
reptile crossly. "I don't understand why

15

you've chained me up like this. You know I'm innocent – thanks to my time machine, you saw the truth with your own eyes, just three days ago!"

"I think you were tricking me somehow," said Bunwinkle. "Now, tell me – did you see an orange-brown stegosaurus come this way?"

Zindi nodded at Teggs. "Only him."

"I'm Captain Teggs Stegosaur," Teggs told her. "This dinosaur looked just like me. He *must've* ducked in here – there's nowhere else he could've gone."

Zindi looked thoughtful. "There is one place he could've gone . . . the future!"

Iggy frowned. "Huh?"

"I knew other dinosaurs would want to test my machine," Zindi explained, "so to demonstrate its power, I've just added a 'send-you-back-five-minutes-in-time' button . . ."

Bunwinkle's eyes narrowed. "Are you suggesting that the second Teggs we saw was the *same* Teggs – visiting from the future?"

"Was he wearing this?" Zindi held up a ridged helmet and a large silver tunic with golden discs stitched onto both arms and up and down the chest.

"Yes!" Teggs stepped forward in amazement. "That's the outfit my double was wearing outside."

"What is it?" Bunwinkle demanded.

Zindi frowned. "What do you mean, what is it? You wore this yourself when you tried out my machine."

"I know that," said Bunwinkle quickly. "I'm only asking so you can explain to our visitors here!"

"Oh. Well, I call it an exo-suit. It protects living things from the powers of the pyramid so they can travel through time safely." Zindi smiled at Teggs. "Looks like the test is going to work – you *are* going to go back in time!"

"Because we've already seen it happen," Arx realized, his horns quivering with excitement.

"Wow, thinking about time travel makes you dizzy! Quick, Zindi, let me put on that exo-suit." Teggs ran over and slipped inside the baggy, tingling material – part costume, part machine. "There!"

"Are you sure it's safe?" Gipsy fretted.

"Don't worry." Zindi pointed to a prominent blue button near the top of the pyramid. "To perform a five-minute time jump, all I have to do is press this. I'll pop your captain into the past for sixty seconds – then bring him back again."

Teggs checked the time on the clock: 18.30. "I'm ready," he said.

Bunwinkle and the astrosaurs watched closely as the machine hummed into life and Zindi hit the blue button. Teggs felt the metal discs on his skin prickle and itch as the world seemed to blur around him . . .

And suddenly only Zindi was in the room – and she had her back to him, absorbed in the workings of her humming, rustling machine. He checked the clock – it now said 18.25.

*I really have gone back into the past!*
Teggs boggled. Quietly he crept out of
the room. Then he galloped down the
corridor, opened the door and burst
outside. With a mind-spinning thrill, he
saw himself, Bunwinkle and his friends
right there in front of him – just as it
had happened five minutes ago.

"It works!" Teggs cried.
"It actually works!" Then
he dodged back into the
corridor and slammed
the door. He felt dizzy
– Zindi had to be pulling
him out of the past. "So
*that's* how I seemed
to vanish from the
corridor . . ."

As he staggered back into
the officers' room, he saw the clock was
again showing 18.30. He had returned
to the present, surrounded by his startled
friends – and the grinning Bunwinkle.

"Amazing!" cried Rosso.

"It certainly was," Teggs agreed, taking off the exo-suit. "What an incredible trip."

"Could I see your machine, Zindi?" asked Arx.

"Stuff off, greenie. I'm having it!" Bunwinkle snatched the suit from Teggs. "I've been waiting to be sure this time machine works – and now I know it does, I'll take it!"

"What?" Teggs turned to the burly governor and saw him shrugging off his uniform – to reveal a big zip running down his middle, and another about his neck.

"That's not Bunwinkle's real skin!" Gipsy's head crest had flushed blue in alarm, and Zindi's eyes were on stalks. "It's only a costume!"

"This is a fake Bunwinkle," cried Rosso. "An impostor in a diplodocus suit!"

Arx frowned. "But then . . . who's inside?"

"Take a look," came a chillingly familiar voice, as "Bunwinkle" unzipped his neck and pulled off his head – to reveal a scuffed, scarred and tiger-striped velociraptor! He wore a black combat suit. A patch covered one eye. And now he reached down inside his costume and pulled out a gun.

"We've got to be seeing things." Teggs stared in horror. "It can't be you!"

"It's me all right, Teggs," hissed the raptor. "Your deadliest enemy – General Loki!"

# Chapter Three

## PLOTS AND PLANS

"What are we waiting for?" growled Iggy. "Let's get that stripy loser."

"Stay back, Iggy," Admiral Rosso ordered. "He's holding an atom gun. It could zap us all to ashes."

Teggs raised his spiky tail and bunched his fists. "Where's the real Bunwinkle, Loki?"

"Lying down in a cupboard in his office," hissed Loki. "I trust you'll agree, my impression of him has been superb."

"You ruthless raptor, how did you get here?" Rosso demanded.

"He was a prisoner, like me," said Zindi, still staring in shock. "Locked up in the cell next door."

"And it was you who put me here, astrosaurs," hissed the scuffed, scaly figure. "Me, Loki – commander of the seven fleets of death! Ruler of the meat mines of Raptos! Killer of kentrosaurus, dominator of dream crystals—"

"And smelliest toilet-breath of the year winner ten times over," Teggs concluded. "How in space did you get hold of a diplodocus costume?"

"Simple." Loki smiled. "Two days ago, I bit one of my warders, who sent me to Bunwinkle's office. The governor was just calling Rosso to arrange your visit to Zindi. But his trip through time had left him so distracted I was able to overpower him the moment he hung up! Then I used his private phone to summon a raptor assault squad – and to call a fancy-dress shop . . ."

Rosso bobbed his head forward. "So you could hire a grey diplodocus costume."

"Precisely," Loki agreed. "I forced Bunwinkle to act normally and hid out in his office till my secret delivery arrived this morning. Perfect timing for Zindi's wonderful demonstration." He snapped his jaws. "Now I shall help myself to my dear neighbour's time machine and destroy you all."

"No!" cried Zindi.

"You can't stop me," Loki sneered.

"Then let's see if *I* can!" Suddenly Teggs lashed out with his fist and thumped the one-eyed raptor on the snout. With a squawk, Loki was knocked right  out of the neck of his diplo-suit. And as he fell, he dropped the gun.

"Get him!" Teggs yelled.

Arx, Iggy and Gipsy started forward at their captain's command. But then the zip down the middle of the abandoned costume opened up, and a dozen vicious-looking black-and-orange reptiles rushed out with horrible speed.

"Raptors!" boomed Rosso in warning. "Must be that assault squad Loki called in. They've been working that diplodocus costume together, like a jumbo pantomime horse!"

But as the evil reptiles began their attack, Teggs rolled onto his back and spun round, knocking three of them to the floor with a single sweep of his spiky tail.

At the same time, Gipsy scooped up Loki's fallen gun – but before she could aim it, another slavering raptor knocked it out of her grip. Gipsy booted the raptor aside, and it staggered straight into a hefty punch from Iggy. At the same time, Arx butted two raptors over to Rosso, who lumbered forward and squashed them under his huge feet.

Teggs dodged another raptor, leaped over the empty diplocostume and landed beside Loki – who was lying face down, apparently cowering in fear. "Give it up, Loki. You're finished."

"Finished?" Loki rolled over to reveal that he now wore a gas mask. "You potato-brained plop-head! *You're* finished . . ." He hurled a white cube down at the floor and it burst open in a hissing haze of smoke.

"Gas!" Teggs gasped. "Look out, everyone!" But already his head was spinning. Within moments the world about him had dwindled to darkness, and he knew no more . . .

"Wake *up*, Captain!" Teggs stirred groggily at the sound of Gipsy's voice. His eyes flickered open and he saw her face looking down at him, full of concern.

"It's all right, sir.

You were closest to the gas so you've slept longer than everyone else. But you're going to be fine . . ."

Suddenly Bunwinkle pushed in beside her.

"Get back!" Teggs cried.

Gipsy shushed him. "Don't worry, this is the *real* Governor Bunwinkle, sir."

Teggs breathed a sigh of relief. "I'm glad you're OK. Where's Loki and his assault squad?"

"I'm afraid they got away," said Bunwinkle. "With the time machine."

"Admiral Rosso's gone straight to DSS HQ and put the whole vegetarian sector on red alert," said Gipsy quickly. "We'll find him."

"Not if he's hiding somewhere in the past," Teggs muttered.

"I'm sorry," said Bunwinkle, helping Teggs to stand. "That wretched raptor threatened to have my grandmother eaten if I tried to warn anyone he'd escaped. Then he knocked me out and tied me up. What could I do?"

"It's what *Loki* could have done that worries me." Teggs shook his dizzy head. "He said he'd destroy us all – so why didn't he?"

"I think he wants us to sweat," said Zindi. She was free of her chains now and working with Arx, hunched over a mass of machinery and wires. "He knows that with a time machine, he can strike whenever he wants."

"Loki literally has all the time in the world," said Gipsy sadly.

Teggs looked about. "Where's Iggy?"

"Stoking the *Sauropod*'s engines," Arx

reported, plugging cables into sockets inside a metal frame in the shape of a pyramid. "Admiral Rosso wants us to be ready to go after Loki as soon as Zindi and I have finished here."

Teggs frowned. "And what are you doing?"

"Building an identical time machine from my notes," said Zindi. "It took me five years to build the first one . . . but with Arx's help and supplies from your ship, the second one should be ready in twenty-four hours!"

"Now"
– Gipsy turned

to Bunwinkle – "we'd better get back to sewing the new exo-suits . . ."

Teggs saw a heap of silvery material stitched through with wires and golden discs, and a pile of half-finished helmets. "You're making replacements for the safety gear Loki took?"

Bunwinkle nodded. "For you and your three friends to wear when you go after him. It's a good thing I'm the reigning champion in the Space Prison Sewing League!"

Teggs smiled weakly. "It looks as if you guys have everything under control. What should I do?"

"I think you should rest until that gas

has completely worn off, Captain," said Gipsy fondly. "Something tells me we're headed for the greatest adventure of our lives!"

Teggs was too worried to rest. As soon as he'd stopped feeling dizzy from the gas, he went to the *Sauropod*'s gym for a workout. His space radio was tuned in to DSS news reports – Rosso had put hundreds of ships on Loki's trail. If only one of them would find something . . .

Suddenly he jumped as a new report squawked from the radio's speakers. "A raptor assault squad has been arrested while trying to escape in sector seven of the Veg-meat Zone."

"YES!" Teggs cheered.

"Unfortunately," the newsreader went on, "General Loki was not among the captured carnivores."

Teggs groaned. "BOOOOOO!"

"However, a heavily shielded raptor death-flyer *has* been sighted in sector eight." The newsreader sounded grave. "It vanished into a small black hole, believed to be a newly-formed tunnel in space . . ."

"A space tunnel!" Teggs breathed. The *Sauropod* had travelled through one before, and had barely survived. Space tunnels were like intergalactic short cuts between two distant points – a hundred-year journey might take mere minutes by space tunnel. But any such voyage was incredibly dangerous – the forces within the tunnel could smash spaceships to smithereens . . .

Teggs pressed a red button on the radio – the hotline to Admiral Rosso. "Hello?" came Rosso's voice.

"Sir, this is Teggs. Do I have permission to

pursue Loki through that tunnel?"

Rosso paused. "Granted," he murmured. "I was just about to contact you. Our experts have interrogated Loki's gang of raptors and  studied that space tunnel they made. And now we know where Loki has gone."

Teggs waited tensely. "Well?"

Rosso took a deep breath. "The space tunnel leads to . . . Planet Earth."

"Earth!" Teggs gasped in awe. "The ancient home of the dinosaurs. But why would Loki want to take a time machine to Earth?"

"None of us know, not even his raptors," Rosso reported. "But you can be sure he has something terrible in mind. Whatever it takes, Teggs – Loki must be stopped!"

## Chapter Four

## THE DINOSAURS OF MARS

Within twelve hours, the astrosaurs had waved goodbye to Zindi and Bunwinkle and were jetting off to the space tunnel in the *Sauropod*.

Everyone inside was hard at work.

Iggy was busy testing the powerful force-field generators he and Arx had installed in each of the ship's six shuttles.

 Together they would create a super-tough invisible shield right around the *Sauropod*.

Arx and a group of iguanodon engineers were checking and double-checking every circuit in the new time machine. "It's an exact copy of the one Loki stole from Zindi," Arx noted. "It's not strong enough to send the whole *Sauropod* back through time, but it should be able to transport a shuttle with a crew of four."

Chirping in agreement, a group of dimorphodon – the *Sauropod's* flying reptile flight crew – flapped around Shuttle Alpha, fitting it with special exo-discs that would keep it safe on the incredible journey ahead.

Meanwhile, Gipsy and Teggs were on the flight deck testing the special exo-suits, snipping at loose stitches and checking that each special disc was in place.

Teggs tried on his own suit. "I shouldn't have eaten those bushes at lunch time!" he groaned, trying to hold in his stomach. "Do we really have to wear these things?"

"If we don't," Gipsy told him, "Zindi said our bodies will be torn apart by raw time energy the moment we try to travel."

Teggs gulped. "We really have to wear these things."

"Warning!" shrieked the alarm pterosaur through speakers around the ship. "Space tunnel dead ahead. Starting to suck us in. SQUAWWWK!"

Teggs looked at Gipsy. "This is it!"

He switched on the scanner screen. Starless blackness gaped ahead of them.

Gipsy switched on her communicator. "All crew stand by for a bumpy ride!"

Arx hurried onto the flight deck and took his seat. "The time machine is ready," he announced. "We can use it as soon as we've travelled through the tunnel."

"Good work," said Teggs. "But are you sure we will be able to find Loki?"

"Zindi built a tracer into her time machine, in case it ever got lost," Arx explained. "Right now its signal shows that Loki has gone back sixty-five million, one hundred thousand and fifty-six years into the past."

Teggs whistled. "That's a long way back."

"But nothing's changed in our own time, has it?" said Gipsy. "Perhaps his ship didn't make it through the space tunnel. Or if it did, perhaps he hasn't been able to do whatever it is he wanted to do."

Arx shook his head. "When an earthquake happens at sea, it creates a tidal wave. It may take many minutes for that wave to strike land, but it hits in the end. And I think a *time*-quake is much the same."

Teggs nodded. "Even now the effects of Loki's meddling – what he'll do  if we *don't* go back and stop him – could be crashing through the centuries towards us . . ."

Iggy's face appeared on the scanner screen. "The space tunnel is pulling us in faster, Captain. Should I put the engines in reverse to slow us down?"

"No, Iggy," said Teggs. "The sooner we're through this thing the better.

Switch on those shuttle shields of yours
and increase our thrusters to maximum
power!"

"Maximum?" Iggy puffed
out his scaly cheeks, then
chuckled. "Right you
are, Captain."

Teggs turned to
Sprite, the dimorphodon's team
leader. "Shut down all but the most
vital systems."

Sprite launched into the air, tweeting
to his fellows as they zoomed and
swooped between the controls, pulling
levers and flicking switches. Lights
winked out and screens went blank as
the *Sauropod* picked up
speed.

"Entering the space
tunnel in five seconds!"
Arx shouted.
"Five . . . four . . .
three . . ."

Teggs wedged himself into his control pit. "Hold on tight, everyone. Here we go!"

As Arx's countdown concluded, the ship shook and started to spin. The air grew hotter. The few remaining lights glared red like STOP signs. But there was no turning back now. Teggs closed his eyes as the *Sauropod* whizzed onwards through the tunnel, creaking and grinding and rattling and stretching. He thought his bones would bounce right out of his skin as the great ship's flight grew wilder, crazier, completely out of control . . .

Then – WHOOOSH!

Glowing red-hot, the *Sauropod* was

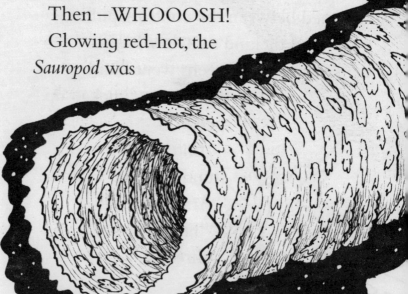

flung out the other end of the tunnel like
a sizzling stone.

"Brakes!" Teggs commanded, as dizzy
dimorphodon fell flapping
all around
him.

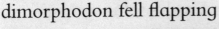

Arx pulled hard on
a big lever, and with a
screeching, scorching rush
of reverse energy, the *Sauropod*
came to a steaming stop.

"Well," said Teggs, clutching his
queasy tum. "That wasn't so bad."

"It was completely horrible," said Gipsy.
"But at least we're still alive."

"Switch all systems on again," said Teggs, climbing out of the scorching-hot control pit. "Did we make it, Arx? Have we come out in Earth's solar system?"

With a wobbly hand, Arx switched on the space radar. "We're just forty million miles away from Earth, sir," he reported. "Close to the planet Mars."

"Wow." Gipsy whistled. "The history books say that the first dinosaurs in space lived on Mars."

"And Venus too," said Arx. "They used up most of the solar system's resources – that's why when the meteor hit Earth, the dinosaurs had to leave this part of space altogether and strike out for somewhere new."

Teggs nodded. "And now, sixty-five million years later . . . we're back!"

"Mars is a dead world now," Arx declared. "The only place around here that can support life is the Earth – and it's full of those funny human things."

Teggs nodded. "I've seen blurry pictures taken through megascopes. They're an odd bunch. I hope they don't spot us in space – they'd most likely try to blow us to bits."

"They won't," Arx assured him. "Human technology is pretty basic. They don't even have proper spaceships."

"Then what is THAT?" Gipsy pointed at the scanner, which had just flickered back into life. It showed a huge, scary spaceship approaching; it was shaped like a double fang and a red skull was stencilled on its side.

"Must be Loki's ship," Teggs murmured. "He can't have had a chance to use the time machine yet."

Arx wasn't sure. "Loki took a shielded death-flyer through the space tunnel, remember? I don't recognize this design."

"Probably a new raptor invention." Teggs turned to Sprite. "Steer us around Mars. When Loki follows us, we'll double back and attack."

The dimorphodon clattered away to obey. But then Gipsy gasped. "Message incoming, Captain — from Mars!"

"But I thought it was a dead planet?" Teggs frowned. "Put the message through."

"This is Martian Dinosaur Command,"  came a low, hissing voice. "Identify yourselves, or our warships will attack."

Gipsy gulped. "Dinosaurs with warships on Mars?"

"Space radar shows there are massive dino-space forts all over the planet," said Arx incredulously. "And loads more on the Earth."

"But what about the humans?" Gipsy quavered.

"Switch on the long-range astro-scopes," ordered Teggs. "Let's have a look at them."

Arx flicked some switches and a blue world swam fuzzily into view. Teggs had seen its picture in history books – now he and his friends gazed out in wonder at the real thing . . .

But as the shuttle's super-telescopes zoomed in on the planet, one thing became very clear.

There *were* no humans on the Earth!

The planet was full of dinosaurs –
*meat-eating* dinosaurs of many different
breeds. Their filthy cities and meat farms
were everywhere.

'Something is very wrong,' Teggs
muttered. "No humans and no plant-
eating dinosaurs. Only carnivores."

"This is Martian Dinosaur Command,"
came the snarling voice again. "You have
been classified as hostile. We will now
destroy you."

"Wait!" said Teggs. "This is an
astrosaur ship on an urgent mission for
the Dinosaur Space Service."

"Astrosaur?" sneered the voice. "What's an astrosaur? And what is the Dinosaur Space Service?"

Teggs tried again. "We've come from the Vegetarian Sector—"

"The what?" Nasty laughter crackled over the speakers. "You'll be telling us you're a ship full of plant-eating dinosaurs next."

"We are!" Teggs shouted. "What's so funny about that?"

"Everyone knows the plant-eaters were wiped out by the great meteor," the voice snarled. "Only us meat-eaters escaped before it hit – and a few thousand years later we came back again."

"What a pathetic attempt to trick us," came another mean-sounding voice. "Don't you know anything about history?"

"Not *this* version of history," said Teggs quietly. "It's been rewritten – by Loki!"

Gipsy's headcrest had flushed pink with shock. "He's started a time-quake sixty-five million years ago, and the aftershocks have destroyed our present! Everything we've ever known ... all our friends ... "

"They no longer exist." Teggs could hardly take it in. "So ... how come *we're* still here?"

"We must have been inside the space tunnel at the moment history changed," said Arx, "and so we were protected."

Teggs gazed out at the terrifying pictures on the scanner. "The last survivors of our own time ..."

Suddenly the *Sauropod* rocked as carnivore missiles exploded all around.

"We won't survive much longer if we

don't get out of here!" yelled Gipsy.

"Call Iggy and tell him to fire up Shuttle Alpha." Teggs whistled to the dimorphodon leader. "Sprite, take evasive action. Keep those Martian meat-guzzlers distracted while Arx, Gipsy, Iggy and I take the time machine – and get on Loki's trail."

Sprite saluted. "Eeep!"

"Thank you." Teggs gave him a crooked smile as the ship shook once again. "I hope I see you again too." As Sprite chirped out orders to his chittering team, Teggs turned to Arx and Gipsy. "Quickly, you three – grab your exo-suits and let's get to the shuttle bay." He took a deep breath, his heart pounding. "I hope that pyramid's fully charged. Our next stop has got to be Earth – in the distant past!"

## Chapter Five

### DOWN TO EARTH

"It's going to be a bumpy ride," Iggy told
Teggs, Arx and Gipsy as they bundled on
board Shuttle Alpha. All four were now
wearing exo-suits and ready for action.
"Stand by for blast-off!"

As the *Sauropod*'s exit hatch slid open,
Teggs saw the blackness of space lit
up by streaks of laser fire and
mega-bright explosions
as the carnivore craft
continued their
attack. "Think
you can steer us
safely through
that lot, Ig?"

"The shuttle's force field took a walloping in the space tunnel. But I'll do my best," Iggy promised. "With luck, those Martian meat-chompers won't even notice us go."

"Activating time machine." Arx switched on the metal pyramid that sat at the back of the shuttle, and it glowed red. The gold discs on the astrosaurs' exo-suits – and on the outside of the shuttle itself – began to glow too. "Power building . . ."

A huge explosion just outside nearly knocked them to the floor. "That was close," said Gipsy shakily. "We could be blown to bits before the pyramid has even warmed up."

"So let's find somewhere a little quieter," yelled Iggy, releasing the brake. "Here we go!"

The shuttle shot away. Gripping the flight stick, Iggy steered with fierce concentration, looping the loop around incoming missiles, veering left and right to dodge the barrage of blasts from the carnivore warship ... Finally Shuttle Alpha broke free of the conflict and zoomed away through the blackness of space towards the green-blue disc of the Earth.

"Well done, Ig." Teggs clapped him on the back and looked down at the pulsating pyramid, which had started to steam. "Arx, how's the time machine doing?"

"Power systems are reaching critical," cried Arx.

"What does that mean?" asked Gipsy.

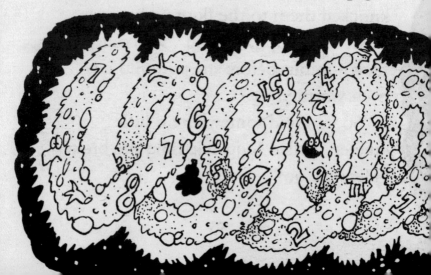

Arx stared helplessly at the machine. "Either it's about to explode and blow us to bits . . . or we're going to make the time-jump!"

Teggs wasn't sure which option was scarier. But the next moment a massive flash of red lightning zapped through his senses. It was a thousand times more powerful than his last little hop through time. The world around him seemed to melt like hot wax. Teggs felt as though he were riding the fastest rollercoaster in the universe, spiralling through the cold infinity of space . . .

BLAMM! Again the crimson light-flash shocked through the shuttle, and suddenly everything seemed back to normal.

"First the space tunnel, then the *time* tunnel," Gipsy groaned. "My poor tummy needs a holiday."

"The time machine's power cells have blown a fuse," Arx fussed, waving at a wisp of smoke coming from the back of the golden pyramid. "I hope I can fix it. If I can't, we'll never get back again."

"We can't waste time worrying about that now." Teggs took off his helmet and exo-suit, and his friends did the same. "The important thing is, we made it!"

Through the windscreen, up close, the Earth hung in space like a perfect blue marble.

"Just think," Iggy murmured. "This is the world where dinosaur life began, all that time ago."

"But we don't know much about our last days on Earth," Arx mused, "or the next few centuries for that matter. The records were long since lost . . ."

Suddenly a vast shining shape swooped

down out of nowhere.

"Look out!" Teggs yelled.
There was a
wrenching
*CLANG!* and
a metal spike
tore through
the side of
the shuttle,
missing Gipsy
by millimetres.
Like a mouse
seized by a
supersonic steel eagle,
Shuttle Alpha was snatched away – and
the astrosaurs were flung in all directions.

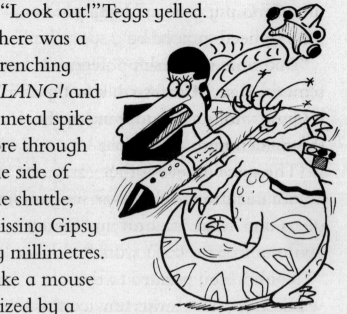

"Our air's escaping!" Teggs yelled.
"Sealing foam, Iggy!"

"On the case." Iggy was already
squirting special airtight foam over the
hole to seal it.

Gipsy glared at the spike. "What is this
thing?"

"It looks like a primitive probe for absorbing star energy," Iggy told her. "We've been speared by a spaceship!"

"But whose spaceship?" Teggs scrambled up. "Can we talk to them?"

Gipsy was already tapping at the shuttle's controls. "No reply."

"The space satellites that carry our communications didn't exist sixty million years ago," said Arx gravely. "So our communicators won't work."

"Look!" Iggy pointed to the windscreen, which was now completely filled by the seas and continents of Earth. "The ship's coming in to land – and taking us with it."

"It looks like we'll soon be meeting the Earth dinosaurs of this time," Teggs murmured. "But who are they, and what are they like?"

Gipsy swallowed hard as they whooshed through the atmosphere. "Looks like we're going to find out – any minute!"

Skewered like a tiny sausage on a colossal cocktail stick, the shuttle broke through a thick bank of clouds and sailed low over a patchwork land of forests and lakes, hills and plains, winding rivers and snow-capped mountains.

Teggs guessed it was towards one of these mountains that they were headed. He glimpsed hundreds of huts and cabins – some kind of settlement. Then the thick whirls of smoky exhaust blocked his view as the spaceship that had spiked them landed on the mountainside.

Almost at once he heard a loud clunk from outside, and then mutterings and whispers.

"What's out there?" hissed Gipsy. "If only this stupid smoke would clear."

Then a spiky figure in a quilted suit and space helmet appeared at the window. The astrosaurs jumped in surprise. Teggs saw that the figure stood on a platform carried by four stout pterosaurs – a kind of flying taxi. Slowly the figure removed his helmet . . .

To reveal a dark green stegosaurus!

Teggs stared in wonder. Dinosaurs had gone on evolving over the last 65 million years, and this stegosaurus was clearly less advanced. He had no hands as such. His legs were thick and solid, his body was bulkier and his backplates were bigger. He looked a formidable sight – but his smile was warm and friendly.

"Hello," the stegosaurus called through the window. "I'm sorry we crashed into you. We didn't see you. It was like you came out of nowhere!"

Teggs smiled wryly. "I suppose we did a bit. Who are you?"

"I'm Zac Stegosaur – community

61

chief, inventor and adventurer." Zac
peered in through the windscreen. "Hey,
this is quite a ship you have, Mr . . ."

"Teggs Stegosaur," said Teggs. "And
I like adventures too! Open the doors,
Iggy." He lowered his voice. "And
remember, we can't let anyone in this
time suspect we're from the future – if
they believed us, it might change history
– so act primitive!"

Iggy flicked a switch and the door slid
open. Coughing on exhaust smoke, the
pterosaurs carried Zac round so

he could climb inside
Shuttle Alpha.
"Wow, I've never
seen technology
like this
before.
Where
did you
get it?" He
frowned

thoughtfully. "You look kind of different from other 'saurs. Where are you guys from?"

"Er . . . we're from all over the place," said Teggs. "Iggy built our ship."

Iggy nodded. "Um, yes. With help from Arx and Gipsy, here."

"I'm pleased to meet you all," said Zac. Then he noticed the crumpled spur of metal sticking out through the wall. "Oh no! Look at my ship's energy-probe. Without that, we can't recharge our power systems in space."

"Don't worry, I can soon mend it," said Iggy. "But what about *our* poor ship?"

"Well, I don't mean to be rude," said Zac, "but while this little ship might look flashy, it's not going to take you far from old Earth, is it? Where are your food supplies? Where are your thousand-years' worth of spare parts? It's just too small – you should think about joining us plant-eaters in the *Soar-a-saurus*."

Teggs frowned. "What's that?"

"The last great hope for all veggie dinosaurs to escape Earth before the meteor hits," said Zac grimly. "I just hope we get her finished before *we're* finished. Six months ago, our telescopes picked up the giant meteor headed our way and we've been building the *Soar-a-saurus* ever since."

"How long before the big rock hits?" asked Gipsy.

"You mean you don't know?" Zac stared in amazement. "We have just a day and a half left. In thirty-six hours, the Earth goes *boom* . . ."

Teggs nodded grimly. "And if Loki isn't stopped, we'll all go *boom* with it!"

## Chapter Six

## CRAFT OF THE FUTURE

"Well, Zac," said Teggs, "I'm not sure we can come with you – but we will certainly help you get your *Soar-a-saurus* ship-shape."

"I can't see at all what shape it is," Iggy complained, peering out through the fading smoke. "But we're a long way up. Are we stuck right at the top of it?"

Zac gave a friendly snort of laughter. "*This* isn't the *Soar-a-saurus*, Iggy. This is just one of the six tug-ships needed to tow her out into space." He pointed through the mist, past the mountain and into the valley beyond. "Look . . . there's the *Soar-a-saurus*!"

Teggs and Gipsy joined Arx and Iggy in the doorway – and all of them gasped. In the distance, a humungous heap of metal sat wedged between two hillsides – an angular spaceship as big as a city! Dinosaurs swarmed over it like specks – fixing, welding, loading, installing . . .

Gipsy boggled. "That thing's ma-hoosive!"

"It needs to be," said Zac. "It's got to hold thousands of plant-eaters as well as eggs from every species, kept frozen and ready to hatch on distant worlds."

"Now I see why you need six super-speedy space tugboats to drag it out of Earth's atmosphere," said Iggy. "It's so big, it could never take off by itself."

"But it'll get all us plant-eaters away," said Zac fiercely. "You'll see. It will work!"

Gipsy put a gentle hoof on his shoulder. "Do some dinos think that it won't?"

Zac sighed. "The carnivores laugh at us because the *Soar-a-saurus* won't run on clockwork power like every other spaceship."

"Clockwork?" Iggy spluttered. "That's crazy!"

But Arx nudged him in the ribs. "This far back in history, most dinosaur machines ran on clockwork."

"You're right, Iggy, it IS crazy," said Zac. "My idea is to run spaceship engines on dung! By burning dung you get powerful gases that can push a spaceship five times as fast . . ."

"Spaceships that run on dung, eh?" Teggs smiled. "You know what, Zac? I think your idea is going to catch on!"

"The carnivores don't think so. They're all leaving the planet in a fleet of clockwork rockets." Zac pointed through the porthole on the other side of the shuttle. "You can see for yourself – their camp's on the other side of the mountains."

Now that the smoke had faded, the astrosaurs could see clear across the landscape in the opposite direction.

Giant spires of blood-red metal stood hard against the sky – and bolted onto the sides were gleaming metal tubes.

"Um . . ." Iggy lowered his voice. "Is it me, or do those tube things look like laser cannons – *modern* laser cannons, from *our* time?"

"They certainly do," Teggs agreed.

"But the history books say that on Earth our ancestors built no weapons," Arx muttered. "They battled with teeth, tails and claws as they had always done."

"There's only one dinosaur who could stick modern lasers onto ancient rocket-ships," said Gipsy.

Teggs nodded. "General Loki. And we're running out of time to stop him!"

Zac and his four powerful pterosaurs took the astrosaurs down to the plant-eater camp on the rickety platform. Teggs thought of the dimorphodon and the rest of his crew, thousands of miles and millions of years away, trapped in a terrifying future that should never have been.

*Hang in there, guys,* Teggs thought. *We'll put things right.*

As the platform was whisked through the sky, it offered a good view of the whole camp. Different dino-breeds of all sizes were working together in the fields, gathering a humongous harvest.

Young hatchlings and old dinos were doing their bit, carrying supplies on board the *Soar-a-saurus* or shovelling dollops of dung into the gigantic engines built into the back of the super–colossal craft. Other pterosaurs were helping too, swooping about with things to be packed and passing messages between different groups.

Teggs was glad to see the *Soar-a-saurus* was well defended. The steep sides of the valley helped to shield it, and a tall metal barrier ran along the hills that faced out over carnivore territory.

"That's an electric fence," Zac explained as they glided over it.

"The carnivores used to sneak in and raid our camp, stealing supplies for their rocket fleet. So I designed that to keep them out."

"You're quite the inventor," Arx observed as they came in to land over a field picked bare of all but a few blades of grass.

Zac shrugged modestly and checked his watch. "I'm just trying to make sure we all get out of here before that meteor hits."

"No wonder everyone's working so hard," said Gipsy as they landed in the mud with a bump.

"I'll arrange another flock of pterosaurs to lift your shuttle off our tug-ship and bring it down here," said Zac. "But I'm afraid I can't spare anyone to help you fix it. I need to repair that tug-ship and test out the other five."

"I'll help you," said Iggy, clambering off the platform with his friends. "I'm good with engines."

"And I'm clever with machines," added Arx.

"We'll take any help we can get," said Zac gratefully.

"And in the meantime, I'd better pay a visit to the carnivore camp," said Teggs.

"What?" Zac gasped. "Are you crazy?"

"I *have* to go," Teggs told him. "You see, when you ran into us in space we were on the trail of a bad-news raptor named Loki. We think he's going to try to stop you leaving."

Gipsy turned to Teggs. "I'd like to go with you, Captain. Loki's too tricky to tackle alone."

"He won't be alone," Teggs reminded her. "He'll have thousands of carnivores with him!"

"I still want to come," Gipsy insisted.

"Really, guys," said Zac. "Tomorrow we'll be leaving Earth. The meat-munchers will be too busy preparing for their own rocket-ride to safety to bother with—" He broke off at the sound of a crash from across the field.

Teggs turned and saw that a pretty yellow stegosaurus with little hatchlings tucked between her backplates was trying to pull a heavy crate with her tail.

"Gazell!" Zac's face creased with concern and he hurried away. "Don't try to carry those spare parts by yourself. Let me help you . . ."

"Arx, Iggy, you try to help too," Teggs said. "Gipsy and I will head off to the carnivore camp and do our best to stop Loki – before something terrible happens!"

Two hours later, as the moon hung like a chewed silver claw in the perfect black of the night, Teggs and Gipsy were nearing their destination. Pausing beside a stream, they noticed a large sign, the words scratched into a sheet of metal:

> **WARNING – Carnivore Camp Ahead.**
> **Plant-Eater Trespassers Will Be Eaten.**
> **Or Scrunched.**
> **Or Splatted.**
> **Or Jumped Up And Down On Until Dead Or Very Unwell.**
> **Then Eaten.**

"Do you think they're trying to tell us something?" said Gipsy nervously.

"I think we need a disguise." Teggs crouched

down beside the stream and picked up
a couple of sharp stones. He stuck them
under his lip so they looked like fangs.
"How's that?" he mumbled.

"Those backplates are a dead giveaway,"
Gipsy informed him. She reached into the
stream and scooped out some mud, then
smothered it over Teggs's back like brown
cement. Soon his spiky back was hidden
beneath a smooth
ridge of dirt.
"Now, if you
walk on your
back legs ..."
Teggs reared
up and offered
Gipsy a couple
more pointed
stones he'd
found. Gipsy
slipped them
in place. "I look
like a walrus!"

"Let's just hope no one looks at us too closely," said Teggs. "Try to act like a meat-eater."

Together they stomped and swaggered past the sign, with the air of dinosaurs who owned the place. Before long, they spotted a pair of huge carnotaurs.

"Guards!" hissed Gipsy.

"Stop!" The biggest carnotaur lumbered over, his friend just behind him. "Who're you?"

Teggs gulped and tried not to lose his teeth. "Er . . . Us come from far away. Want to ride in rocket."

"You're nearly too late," snarled the second carnotaur. "What's the password?"

"Um . . . password?" Gipsy looked nervously at Teggs.

"All meat-eaters know the password. No password, no rocket-ride off the Earth." The biggest carnotaur loomed over them, his claws twitching. "And we will eat you alive for wasting our time. What is the password?" His drool-soaked jaws opened wider. "WHAT?"

## Chapter Seven

### CAMP OF FEAR

As the two carnotaurs hissed and growled, Teggs racked his brain for a possible password . . .

Suddenly Gipsy's bottom made a rude noise!

The biggest carnotaur stopped snarling, sniffed – and grinned. "Yep, that's the password all right!" He and his friend stood aside. "You can go."

"Phew!" Teggs grabbed the blushing Gipsy and hurried away up a hillside. "Nice work, Gipsy."

"Thank my bottom," Gipsy whispered. "I was so scared I couldn't control it – luckily for us."

Teggs nodded. "Let's hope our luck holds."

As the astrosaurs reached the crest of the hill, Teggs surveyed the carnivore camp. It was a far cry from the rusting, fume-filled, high-rise cities of his time. These primitive meat-eaters had set up a sprawling mess of grubby big-tops and tents and tepees stretching out for miles, all in the shadow of the line of chunky blood-red rockets.

Stealthily Teggs and Gipsy made their way down the slope and into the noisy, smelly heart of the camp. It was like a colossal carnivore carnival, with tribal drums booming and barbecues blazing.

"Trust this brutal bunch to be celebrating the end of the world," Gipsy muttered.

"I can't see Loki's death-flyer," said Teggs. "We'll have to search the whole area."

All breeds of meat-eater were crushed into the grotty tents, drinking swamp beer and fighting over food. The stench of dung and meat was everywhere. A T. rex came staggering out of a tent. "Roll up!" he rasped. "See Trixie the belly dancer! She'll be dancing with the chopped-off belly of a diplodocus!"

Teggs felt sick. "No, thanks."

"Have your future told by Madame Hagburger," leered a wrinkled oviraptor. He gestured to an old dinosaur in a filthy cloak with a cracked crystal ball, talking to a megalosaurus.

"I see you is going to be hit on the head," said Madame Hagburger – before socking her customer with a big stick.

As the megalosaurus groaned and fell over, Teggs and Gipsy jumped over his body and hurried on.

But suddenly there was a fanfare of trumpets close by and the loud music stopped abruptly. "Make way for the King!" came a growling shout. "Behold, King Rokol . . . and the Great Star Raptor!"

"Great Star Raptor?" Gipsy cringed. "That can only be—"

"Loki!" Teggs hissed as the crowds parted to reveal two dinosaurs sprawled on huge crimson sedan chairs, each carried by a pair of sweating T. rexes.

Loki lounged in one, resplendent in his black leather uniform, and in the other lay a vast maroon spinosaurus, a golden crown perched on his head and scarlet robes tight about his body. Slowly he rose to his taloned feet.

"Hear me, my subjects," King Rokol shouted. "It's the last night for Planet Earth. And our honoured guest, the Great Star Raptor, has shared with me a fiendishly flesh-licious plan."

"Indeed I have!" Now Loki rose from his seat. "As you know, I have already given you amazing weapons for your rockets that will allow you to conquer anyone you meet in space. How cool am I?"

"Very cool!" came the riotous response.

"Exactly!" Loki flung open his arms. "Now I say to you – why not test them out here on Earth – by using them against the plant-eater camp?"

Unhappy murmurings went up about the camp.

"Use machines to slay plant-scoffers instead of our teeth and claws?" cried a troodon. "That's not the meat-eater way."

King Rokol stood up with some difficulty. "The Star Raptor means that we can destroy their stupid electric fence with the new weapons."

Teggs and Gipsy swapped worried looks as the snarling, spitting crowd around them grew snarlier and spittier.

"That's right!" Loki yelled. "And while the plant-eaters panic, *we* shall attack. Why should those puny plant-eaters get away from the meteor when they can get in our stomachs?"

"Begin the bombardments!" boomed Rokol as the carnivores waved and cheered. "Once the way is clear, we shall catch and scrunch every last leaf-licker we can find!"

As Loki and the king were swept triumphantly away at the head of the braying meat-munching mob, Teggs put his communicator to his lips. "Arx, Iggy, can you hear me?"

"That won't work," Gipsy reminded him. "We're in the past, remember?"

"Of course." Teggs scowled. "Well, if we can't warn the plant-eaters, our only hope is to smash Loki's weapons before they smash the camp. Come on!"

He and Gipsy started pushing against the tide of carnivores rushing towards the exit.

"Get out of my way!" growled a huge allosaur.

"You get out of ours!" Teggs tried to barge past the brutal meat-eater, but there was a scuffle – and the chunks of mud hiding Teggs's  backplates started crumbling away.

"Look out, Captain!" Gipsy couldn't help but shout – and as she did so, her false fangs fell out.

"Hey!" The big allosaur frowned at Teggs and Gipsy. "You're pretty funny-looking carnivores."

A young T.rex bundled up. "They not meat-eaters. They is *leaf-nibblers*!"

"We've been rumbled," squealed Gipsy.

"Plant-eaters!" someone bellowed. "Spies! Here in our camp!"

"Catch them!" came a blood-curdling cry. "*Eat* them!"

"Quick, Gipsy!" Teggs dragged her away and barged through the crowd of scowling, snarling meat-eaters all around them. His tail brushed against a huge flap of fabric – and he quickly tore it open. "Into this tent!"

Only once Teggs had ducked inside did he realize the dark and stinking tepee belonged to Madame Hagburger the fortune-teller. She was flossing her sharp teeth with a rusty hacksaw and scowled at her unexpected visitors.

"I'm having a tea break," she snapped. "Push off."

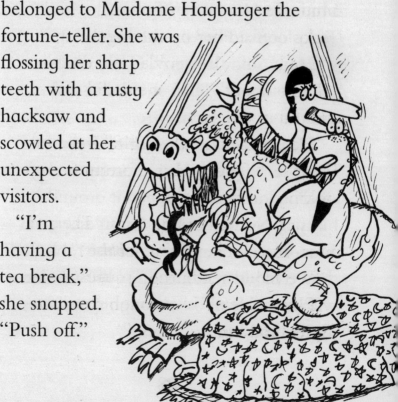

"But we're here to read *your* future," said Teggs quickly. "I see a big tail approaching your face at high speed . . ."

Madame Hagburger frowned – and Teggs conked her on the head.

"Hey," said the grizzled old dinosaur. "You're good!" Then she slid to the ground in a deep snooze.

"Hide her under the table," Teggs told Gipsy as he grabbed the fortune-teller's smelly cloak and wrapped it around himself. No sooner had Gipsy dragged Madame Hagburger under the tablecloth than a blood-red baryonyx burst inside with a rabble of other tough carnivores just behind him.

"Seen a couple of plant-eaters come in here?" he growled.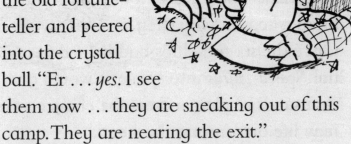

Teggs tried to impersonate the old fortune-teller and peered into the crystal ball. "Er . . . *yes*. I see them now . . . they are sneaking out of this camp. They are nearing the exit."

"We'll see about that," growled the baryonyx, as he turned and charged away. "Come on, you lot – let's go!"

Gipsy poked her head out from beneath the table. "Looks like meat-eaters were even stupider sixty-five million years in the past!"

"Lucky for us." Teggs got up. "Now, we must reach those carnivore rocket-ships – and make Loki's future weapons history!"

★

Back at the plant-eater camp, Iggy had taken a break from repairing Shuttle Alpha to check out the *Soar-a-saurus*'s whopping engines. The super-ship's power systems were an incredible lash-up, using random spare parts from dino-cars and trucks and cycles – but Iggy could find no reason why they wouldn't work. Once the six tug-ships had helped to tow the *Soar-a-saurus* into space, it would give thousands of plant-eaters the chance of a new life out among the stars.

"Hello, Mister." Zac's friend, Gazell the yellow stegosaurus, came into the power room, her hatchlings still squashed between her backplates. "How's it looking here? Find anything wrong?"

"No." Iggy smiled. "This ship should handle well, Gazell. I've checked the systems and they're all in working order. They just need a little oil."

"Aha." Gazell looked at her hatchlings. "Kids? Oil time!"

Iggy
blinked
as the
babies on
her back
produced oil-
cans from under
their blankets.
Holding them
with their tails,
they eagerly squirted
the ramshackle workings.

Gazell smiled to see Iggy
so astonished. "I'm from a whole family
of mechanics," she said. "Fixing engines
is in our blood!" Suddenly one naughty
hatchling started squirting *without* a can!
"Henri, that is not oil – don't be so dirty!"

Iggy smiled. "What are your nippers'
names?"

"Henri, Jim, Terry, Morris and . . ." She
frowned. "You know, I just can't decide
on a name for my youngest boy. It bugs

me day and night . . ." She sighed. "You know, I think I'm just trying to distract myself from how scary everything is right now. I used to fix up broken buses – now I'm supposed to fly the biggest spaceship in history!"

"Have you had a chance to test-drive the *Soar-a-saurus*?" Iggy wondered.

"Nope," Gazell admitted. "I'm just gonna close my eyes, cross my legs and hope I don't do what Henri just did!" She shook her head. "We dinos should've prepared for space travel a whole lot sooner."

Iggy remembered what Arx had said. "Some dinos went to Venus and Mars, didn't they?"

"Sure, the Triassic beasts struck out into space," said Gazell. "And the sea-reptiles left to live on the moons of Jupiter a couple of centuries back, fed up with the carnivores trying to get them all the time . . . But I'm talking about *deep* space travel. We've already exhausted the solar system. And after the meteor hits, the Earth won't be back to normal for ages and ages. Zac says we've got to fly much further out, into the unknown . . . on a journey that'll last more than a million years . . ."

"And which will lead you into the Jurassic Quadrant," Iggy murmured. "Zac is right. It's what you have to do."

"Of course he's right," Gazell said. "He's brilliant! Since my husband was eaten by a gang of T. rexes last year, Zac has looked after me and my kids really well."

"I'm glad to hear it," said Iggy with a smile. "Good mechanics are hard to find!"

"So are test pilots." Arx came in, looking pleased. "Luckily, Zac is great! He and I have been testing the other five tug-ships. Once you've helped finish repairs to that one we hit, this amazing craft should be ready to fly!"

But suddenly a deep, muffled thunderclap shook through the *Soar-a-saurus*. Gazell jumped and her hatchlings nearly fell off her back. "What was that?" Another, louder explosion rocked the room, and metal tiles clattered from the walls and ceiling.

"Something's wrong," said Arx, charging from the room. "We'd better get outside. It sounds like we're under attack!"

## Chapter Eight

## CHAOS AT THE CAMP

When Iggy and Arx emerged with Gazell from the depths of the *Soar-a-saurus*, they found the sky alight with mega-bright streaks of ruby-red destruction – coming from the direction of the carnivore camp. Fires were breaking out all around. Distressed dinos were running round in a panic.

"Loki's firing his weapons," Iggy realized grimly.

KA-ZIZZ! The electric fence shook and sparked as red rays zapped against it. THTOOM! One whole section of the fence was blown apart . . . and the pieces smashed down on the cockpit of one of the tug-ships.

"No!" cried Gazell. "We can't lose our only way off this world . . . We *can't*!"

In the middle of the smoke and flames, a frantic Zac was directing the survival effort. "Pterosaurs, try to blow out the flames by flapping your wings really hard . . . You plateosaurus there, beat back the fires with blankets. Diplodocus, *stamp* out the flames – or try a well-aimed wee!"

Iggy, Arx and Gazell rushed up to help. When Zac saw Gazell he frowned. "It's not safe here. Take the children and find somewhere to hide."

Gazell shook her head. "I'll fetch the first-aid supplies and the doctors and nurses."

As she bravely ran off into the smoke with her hatchlings, Iggy and Arx watched the huge electric fence spit blue sparks high into the night and start to collapse completely.

"What are we going to do?" asked Iggy. "Loki's weapons are already taking out the fence.

They could
wreck the *Soar-
a-saurus* too—
OOF!"

A laser blast
nearby threw
Arx into Iggy,
knocking them both to the ground.
"We've got to reach Shuttle Alpha," said
Arx. "Quickly! It's our only chance."

"But the shuttle doesn't have any
weapons," Iggy protested. "What are we
going to do?"

"We're going to hope my wild plan
works out," said Arx grimly. "If it
doesn't, this entire place will go up in
smoke ... and all our futures with it!"

Teggs carried Gipsy on his back as they
made their way towards the rockets. She
made sure to keep Madame Hagburger's
enormous cloak wrapped around them
both. Luckily – if you could call it that

– most carnivores had already fled their camp to get to the plant-eaters . . .

"I can't see a thing," Teggs complained through the smelly material. "Are we nearly there, Gipsy?"

"Yes." Gipsy could see the giant rockets towering ahead, their bolted-on weapons spitting laser bolts. "But there's no one firing the guns."

Teggs peeped out and saw a heavily armoured ship parked beside the red rockets. "There's Loki's death-flyer. Perhaps there's something inside we can use to destroy those weapons."

They hurried across to the death-flyer. The door was locked – but couldn't withstand a combined attack from the two angry astrosaurs. Once inside, Teggs scanned the controls. A black-and-yellow box had been wired messily into the main systems.

"That looks like a remote control unit," said Gipsy. Looking more closely, she saw that one button was labelled LASERS – and that it was switched on. "Hey! Loki must be controlling those weapons from here!"

"Makes sense," said Teggs. "Loki wouldn't want to hand over control of his weapons to Rokol, in case Rokol decided to get rid of him. So he's running the show from here." He fiddled with the black-and-yellow box. "But if we can just get those lasers to *reverse* their fire . . ."

Gipsy grinned. "You mean, so they fire into themselves? That would make them go—"

BANG! One after the other, Loki's lasers blew themselves apart, scorching the rockets they were bolted to. Then Teggs clobbered the remote control unit with his tail – and it exploded in white smoke.

"You did it!" Gipsy cried.

"But those lasers are bound to have done some damage, and there are still hundreds of carnivores racing towards the plant-eater camp," said Teggs worriedly. "How can we possibly stop them?"

Back at the plant-eater camp, Iggy was running through the smoke-filled camp, helping dinosaurs to safety – either getting them inside the *Soar-a-saurus* or hiding them behind the hunks of scrap metal lying around. No one in this time had ever seen a laser before or felt its effect. To them, such sheer power was terrifying – almost as terrifying as watching months of hard work being wrecked in minutes.

"Come on, Arx," Iggy muttered. "Your plan has just *got* to work!"

Then Iggy heard Zac's voice booming through the darkness. "It's not fair! Stop!" Suddenly he saw the stegosaurus, bellowing up at the smoky sky. "We were so close to escaping, so close to a new life. Stop raining fire on us! Stop!"

Iggy ran to him. "Er, Zac? I think the bombardment *has* stopped. Listen!"

An eerie hush had settled over the camp. There were no more zaps of energy, no more explosions. Timid plant-eaters began to poke their heads out from their makeshift shelters. Mothers and fathers comforted their frightened children.

"Thank goodness." Zac saw some large pterosaurs flap overhead. "Grab some torches and check out all the tug-ships and the *Soar-a-saurus*," he yelled. "Whatever's been damaged, we have less than a day to get it fixed."

Then a breathless pterodactyl swooped in to land beside them. "Carnivores sighted!" she squawked. "I spotted them from the air. Hundreds and hundreds of them – looking really fierce and headed this way!"

"But . . . the electric fence is all in bits." Zac groaned. "What can we do? First the carnivores softened us up. Now they're moving in for the kill!"

Iggy turned and shouted back the way he'd come. "Arx! Don't stop the work! The camp's got some uninvited dinner guests on the way – and we're the dinner!"

"What work?" said Zac. "What do you mean?"

But before Iggy could reply, the pterodactyl squawked at ear-splitting volume: "They're coming!"

Iggy and Zac peered through the haze of smoke and saw a seething sea of shadowy shapes surging down the hillside towards the camp. At their head were two elevated figures being carried on grand chairs.

"There's Loki,"

Iggy muttered. "There's nothing he loves more than a bit of destruction."

"And King Rokol too," said Zac. "So the meat-eaters win at last."

And then a small silver shape shot into sight over the dark haze of the hillside.

It was Loki's death-flyer!

Inside the stolen raptor ship, Gipsy peered out of the window while Teggs fought with unfamiliar controls to keep their flight steady.

"Carnivores right below us, Captain," called Gipsy. "They're almost at the camp. What are we going to do? We've blown up all Loki's weapons – now we've got none to use ourselves."

"We can use this whole *ship* as a weapon!" Teggs gave her a dangerous grin. "I'll take us in low ..."

Gipsy gulped as the flyer dipped sharply and accelerated away – heading straight for King Rokol and Loki on their elevated sedan chairs. Both meat-scoffers turned in angry astonishment as Teggs gave a cheeky wave through the windscreen – then whooshed right over their heads. The enormous rush of wind as he passed by knocked both his targets out of their portable thrones. They landed with twin crunches on the ground below. "YEOWW-OOF!"

"Result!" Teggs cried.

"What about the rest of this rotten rabble?" asked Gipsy.

"Take the controls and I'll see what I

can do." As Gipsy gripped the flight stick, Teggs jumped up and crossed over to the flyer's cargo hold. "I think it's time those meat-heads learned what it's like to be bombarded from above!"

He opened the hold's outer doors. Then, bracing himself in the fierce gale, he curled his tail around a crate full of frozen meat and emptied it over the carnivores racing at the front of the pack. Some were struck and fell, others skidded to a stop and started chomping down the free food – only to be trampled and tripped over by the mass of meat-eaters behind.

"You might as well have the box, too!" Teggs yelled as he hurled the empty crate down at the crowd,

107

flattening a few more flesh-munchers. Then he hooked his tail spikes onto another crate, filled with electronic equipment. Hauling it over, he emptied the heavy machinery down on the ravenous dinos! Dozens were conked on the head and fell, flailing about in alarm.

But with a sinking heart, Teggs realized he couldn't hope to stop the sheer number of crazed carnivores racing towards Zac's camp.

"That meat-mad mob have almost reached the veggie camp!" Gipsy wailed. "The fence is in pieces – and any second now, the plant-eaters will be in pieces too!"

## Chapter Nine

## WALKING ON AIR

In the smoking fields of the plant-eater camp, Iggy and Zac watched helplessly as hordes of hate-filled carnivores stormed through the gaps in the electric fence.

Iggy was glad most of the plant-eaters were still sheltering from the laser-storm. That wouldn't save them from the invading carnivores

– but at least they wouldn't know what was coming. "Right then, Zac!" he said gruffly. "If we're going down, let's go down fighting!"

Zac nodded and flexed his spiky tail, ready to rumble. The ravenous rabble of carnivores charged closer and closer . . .

And then – WHAMM!

It was as if they had slammed into an invisible wall. POMM! BAMM! PHOOM! Again and again the carnivores clonked into a barrier that Zac and Iggy couldn't see. More and more meat-eaters came piling in, squashing the ones who'd crashed into the solid air first – then crashing into it themselves.

Zac stared. "I don't get it. What's happened?"

"*Arx* happened!" cried Iggy as a weary but relieved-looking green triceratops ran towards them. "You did it, Arx. You managed to boost the shuttle's force field . . ."

"Just about," Arx agreed. "I rewired the power systems and inflated the ship's energy shield until it covered the entire camp like a protective dome."

Zac gazed in wonder as the crushed-up carnivores bit and snapped at each other, struggling to get clear of the invisible barrier. Then he turned to Arx and bowed. "I don't know who you really are, or where you've come from, or *how* you've done it – but you've saved the camp!"

"And look up there!" Arx pointed

to Loki's death-flyer as it zoomed overhead, with two familiar figures waving through the windscreen. "It's Gipsy and Captain Teggs!"

Iggy grinned. "I wondered what that

raptor ship was up to. The captain must've stolen it."

But suddenly the flyer spun round and round, like a raptor chasing its tail.

"What are they doing?" Arx wondered. "It's as if they've lost control . . ."

"I've lost control, Gipsy!" Teggs cried, wrestling with the flyer's flight stick. "This thing's not doing what I'm telling it to do!"

"I think it's starting to do what *Loki* wants." Gipsy pointed out through the window. "Look!"

Teggs saw that Loki was back in his sedan chair, wielding a large silver handset. "It wasn't only the rocket weapons he designed to work by remote control. He's got power over this whole flyer – and he means to use it!"

"Of course," groaned Gipsy, helping Teggs grip the flight stick. "He couldn't take his raptors through time with him because he only stole one exo-suit – so he had an automatic pilot built in. Can we smash it like you smashed the weapons remote control?"

"It'll be built into the heart of the ship," said Teggs. "We'll never get to it in time." Suddenly the flight stick snapped off in his hand in a fizz of green sparks. "Uh-oh, that's torn it. Time to abandon ship!"

Gipsy's headcrest flushed electric blue. "We can't, we're too high up! We'll be squished!"

"There are still some crates left," shouted Teggs, stumbling dizzily to a couple of shiny boxes in the cargo area. "I think they're made of mega-metal. If we get inside one, it should cushion our fall!"

Gipsy scrambled into one of the crates, which was half full of electrical bric-a-brac. Teggs pushed it over to the open doorway, squeezed his upper body into the box next to Gipsy, and curled his tail against the floor like a giant spring. As the ship stopped spinning and began to move away under Loki's control, Teggs launched himself, Gipsy and the crate into empty space . . .

"Whoaaa!" Gipsy helped pull Teggs into the crate beside her. Neither of them knew where they were, or how high up, or how many carnivores were waiting to get them down below, or if the crate would even protect them from their crash landing . . .

But after only a couple of seconds – POMM! The big metal box crunched against something solid.

"Ooof!" Teggs and Gipsy were thrown out of the crate like jack-in-the-boxes . . .

And found themselves sprawled out in thin air, high above the plant-eater camp!

"Captain! Gipsy!" Arx yelled up at them. "You've landed on my force field!"

115

Teggs beamed down at his friends below. "Better than landing on our butts!"

Then a fierce and furious roar from King Rokol silenced the squashed and squabbling carnivores forced up against the force field.

"Newcomer from the stars," he hissed, rounding on Loki. "You promised us a wonderful night of battle, bloodshed and bone-chewing with your amazing weapons . . . but the plant-eaters have thwarted you and tricked us all. We haven't had so much as a nibble!"

"And you won't, either!" Teggs bellowed. "The star-raptor's weapons are weak compared to the powers of the . . . um . . ."

"The interplanetary plant-eaters!" said Gipsy quickly.

"Right!" Zac bellowed. "With our friends beside us, we're stronger than you meat-bloated bozos will ever be!"

"Curse you, astrosaurs!" Loki yelled.

"See how your mighty star-raptor fears us?" Arx joined in.

"Never forget, these veggie dinosaurs are well-defended." Teggs nodded at King Rokol. "And if you're not careful, we will attack YOU!"

"Nooo!" screeched an allosaurus, weeing himself in fright.

"They have supernatural powers!" a dryptosaurus sobbed. "They'll destroy us all!"

Rokol scowled at Loki. "What a rubbish end to our last day on Earth!" Angry growls of agreement went up from the carnivores all around. "We shall return to our own camp at once."

"Wait!" Loki had finally got full

control over his death-flyer, which hovered overhead like a giant metal hawk. "Please, your majesty. Ride with me in my, er, star chariot, so that I may share other plans with you."

"No!" Rokol declared. "Two of those interplanetary plant-eaters have been inside, and I bet they've left terrible traps. I shall be carried in my great throne as always. *You* can do what you like." With that – and a few barked commands at the chair bearers – he was taken on his teetering way, the carnivore crowds following in his wake.

Loki glared coldly at Teggs and Gipsy. "You haven't won yet. Just you wait!" And he brought his ship down low and scrambled inside.

Moments later the flyer soared away.

"I thought he'd never leave," said Teggs, watching as the other carnivores scuttled away over the hills and vanished into the night. "But now that he has – how are we going to get down from here?"

"You may not have to wait long, Captain," said Arx as the invisible shield began to wobble. "I had to boost the shuttle's force field to the limit, and any moment now it could go—"

POP! Suddenly Teggs and Gipsy were falling again. Iggy ran and caught Gipsy – while Teggs landed in a muddy puddle with a splash.

"Welcome back," said Arx happily.

"There's no time to waste on words." Teggs jumped up, shook himself dry and marched over to Zac. "We've only got tonight to put things right if you're going to leave before the meteor hits."

"It's no good," said Zac quietly. "I mean, thank you for all you've done to help us, but it's hopeless."

He pointed up at a bright orange star in the sky. "Look, there's the meteor. It's going to destroy almost all life on the planet. And because I didn't protect this camp well enough, it's going to destroy us too."

"No way!"

Zac and the astrosaurs started at the loud, shrill voice. It belonged to Gazell, who was leading a long trail of fellow plant-eaters out of the battle-scarred *Soar-a-saurus*. Teggs could see nurse dinosurs with first-aid boxes, mechanics with tools clamped in their mouths, builders in hard-hats made from hollowed-out stone . . . More and more plant-eaters came crowding out, dinosaurs who knew that it was their destiny to reach for the stars – or to die in the attempt.

"You've done so much for us, Zac," said Gazell. "You've looked after us, you've given us a way off this world and you've never let us down. We're not going to let *you* down now by allowing some dumb meteor to use us as target practice. We're going to work hard to

fix this, and we're all going to work together." Her face softened as she smiled at Zac. "That is, if it's OK with you . . . Chief?"

Zac looked at Teggs. "But you and your friends are the ones who saved this camp. You should take charge – not me."

Teggs shook his head and lowered his voice. "These dinosaurs need a strong leader to help them through all the dangers and hardships of the voyage ahead. And believe me, they need *you* to be that leader." He spoke more loudly: "You're the one in charge, Zac. Tell us what to do, and we'll do it."

Zac gave him a grateful smile. "Well, Arx and Iggy are fantastic with machines. Could they lead a work party fixing the damage to the tug-ships, while you and Gipsy help Gazell organize repairs to the *Soar-a-saurus*? We'll need a full report on

everything that's been damaged. Oh, and
we should take a register, too, to make
sure no one is missing."

"We'll work all night," Gazell promised,
and her hatchlings nodded too. "Won't
we, everyone?"

Cries of eager agreement rose up into
the night.

*If all goes well,* thought Teggs, *this will be
the final night of dinosaurs on the Earth. But
if it doesn't . . .*

He shivered as Loki's last words
echoed in his head: *You
haven't won yet. Just
you wait!*

## Chapter Ten

## AN UNEXPECTED GIFT

The orange pinprick of the approaching meteor burned in the dark sky like an omen of doom. Even as dawn broke over the plant-eater camp, it lingered high overhead.

Not a single plant-eater was idle down on the Earth. With just six hours to go before impact, there was still too much to do.

Teggs yawned and stretched, then got back to hammering rivets into the side of the newly-repaired *Soar-a-saurus*. A ragbag

124

team of dino-teens
and old timers
were pushing
them into
place for Teggs
to clobber with
his tail.

He looked
around. Iggy
and Arx were just overseeing the final
work on the tug-ships. Gazell and some
friends were loading the last crates of
food and supplies on board. A gaggle of
triceratops students – their horns dipped
in ink and with large slates to write on –
had been visiting the thousands of cabins
on board the enormous ship, making sure
that all the passengers were safely inside
and ready to go; now Gipsy was checking
their findings.

Zac bustled up to Teggs, looking
absolutely whacked. "How are we doing
here?"

Teggs walloped the last of the rivets. "Finished!"

"And not a moment too soon," said Zac. "Well done, you guys."

Gipsy came along. "Well, Zac, we've counted five hundred thousand, eight hundred and ninety-nine dinos on board. The rest are all out here finishing work. All the eggs are on board, and the dino-gym is fully equipped so that everyone can keep fit on the voyage."

"Thanks, Gipsy," said Zac. "I'm beginning to think we might just get off this planet in time after all."

"But we have trouble, Zac," said Gazell, and the hatchlings on her back wriggled around. "The farmers have been checking the harvest. Those awful red lights last night set fire to half our food supplies. We'll have starved before we reach the nearest star!"

"Can't you grow plants on board the *Soar-a-saurus*?" asked Teggs.

"Yes, but there are thousands to feed, and the plants will take time to grow," Zac explained.

"Perhaps you can stock up again at a nice planet along the way," said Gipsy.

Zac shook his head. "There isn't one. The worlds of the solar system are not as abundant as the Earth. The reptiles in local space can barely feed themselves – we were planning to collect them on our way out."

Gazell pointed past them. "Well, right now we've got a worse problem. Look!"

Zac groaned, and the astrosaurs stared in dismay at the sight of a familiar figure in a sedan chair appearing over the hilltop once again.

"King Rokol and his carnivores," Gipsy whispered. "They're back!"

"What do they want now?" Teggs saw that Loki was not with Rokol this time – and nor was his wild rabble of followers. Instead, a procession of twenty-four hefty meat-stuffers of various breeds came alongside Rokol, each carrying five huge

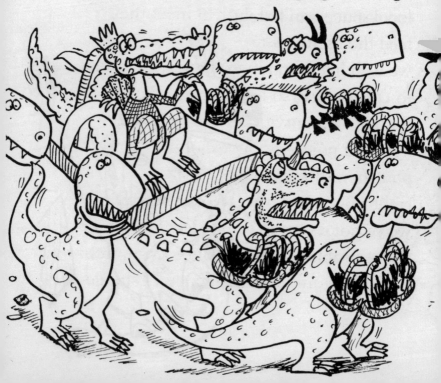

baskets. And in the baskets were . . .

"Plants?" Teggs stared in astonishment. "Are those meat-eaters bringing *plants*?"

Alerted by the cries, Arx and Iggy came charging over from the tug-ships to join Teggs and Gipsy.

"What is Rokol playing at?" wondered Iggy.

"Get everyone inside, Gazell," said Zac firmly. "I'll see what the carnivores want this time."

While Gazell got busy, Zac and the astrosaurs walked over to meet the sharp-toothed king.

"Hear me, plant-eaters – you have nothing to fear!" called Rokol. "I come with gifts for you all."

"Gifts?" Teggs looked suspicious.

"It's true," Rokol insisted, gesturing to his slaves to set him down a safe distance away from the camp's broken fence. "I should never have listened to that fool Loki from the stars. But last night . . . well, you know how it is. We'd finished our packing, we had cool new weapons to try out, we had a few cups of swamp beer too many and got a bit carried away trying to squish you and blow you all up. But the thing is — we're sorry."

Zac raised his eyebrows. "Really?"

"Really!" Rokol bowed his head. "When you and your interplanetary plant-eaters demonstrated your strength and special powers . . . I was impressed, and so were my people."

Rokol's slaves nodded, staring at Teggs and Gipsy. "You walked on the air!" said one.

"You built invisible walls," said another, looking at Arx and Iggy.

"And you destroyed the magic weapons of the weakling star raptor." Rokol shuddered. "I do not wish to see these powers used against us — especially since

we can't hurt
you back with
our rocket lasers
destroyed. So!
As a peace
offering, we
would like you
to accept these."

The king
snapped his
claws and his
subjects came forward
to place the baskets of
potted plants in front of Zac.

"These . . . these are garga-weeds!" Zac
stared in amazement. "The more you eat,
the faster they grow – which is why the
carnivores destroyed most of them."

"Of course," boomed Rokol. "There
are quite enough plant-eaters about
already—" He broke off and forced a
chuckle. "But we have learned the error
of our ways. And so, now we give them

to you freely – as long as you promise to leave us alone."

"We'll see about that," said Iggy. "It could be a trick."

"This gift might be poisoned!" Gipsy agreed.

"Let me examine them," said Arx. "I'm a bit of an expert on plants."

"And I'm an expert at eating them!" said Teggs, his tum rumbling.

The carnivores cringed as Teggs and Arx approached, and pushed forward their baskets.

Arx picked out one of the thick, sticky plants and sniffed its yellow flowers. Then he turned to Teggs and lowered his voice. "I read that garga- weeds grew here on old Earth

but were lost on the great journey into space."

Teggs couldn't resist – he nibbled a leaf – and sure enough, another grew to replace it. "Mmmm!" The garga-weed tasted super-delicious. "It doesn't *seem* to be poisoned." He tried another leaf from another plant in another basket. And another. And another! "Mmm, lovely . . ."

Gipsy grinned. "Save some for Zac, Captain!"

Zac looked up at King Rokol. "Thank you for this kind gift. We shall, er . . . let you leave Earth."

"Phew!" Rokol smiled again as his servants put down their baskets. "I am glad we will know a new age of peace – at least while we journey out through space." He signalled to his slaves, who lifted him in his chair and carried him off. "Farewell!"

Rokol's band followed on behind without a backward glance. Soon, all of them were out of sight.

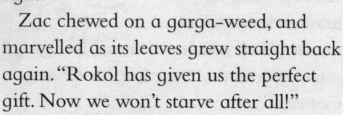

Zac chewed on a garga-weed, and marvelled as its leaves grew straight back again. "Rokol has given us the perfect gift. Now we won't starve after all!"

Arx beamed. "I'll run a couple of tests on these to make sure they're definitely all right . . ."

"And then we must help your passengers get ready for lift-off in the *Soar-a-saurus*," said Teggs excitedly. "There's not much time left, but they'll make it after all – together with a never-ending lunch!"

Within half an hour, Arx had tested leaves from each enormous basket and declared them all safe. Gazell wasted no time in organizing a work party to heave the haul on board. Then the astrosaurs joined Zac in the control room of the biggest tug-ship.

It was like a huge cube split into three levels. The controls were massive, built mainly into the floor so that the dinosaurs could work them with their clumsy feet. A large pterosaur was perched beside an enormous steering wheel, ready to work it with her beak.

"This is like standing inside an antique," Iggy murmured, gazing around. "Fantastic!"

"Once the tug-ships have pulled the *Soar-a-saurus* out into space, Gazell will take full control," Zac explained. "The tug-ships will then join onto the *Soar-a-saurus* and their energy probes will help power her systems. We can also use them as our shuttle craft for visiting new worlds."

"It's going to be an incredible adventure," said Teggs, ushering his crew towards the exit ladder. "I wish we could share it with you."

Zac looked puzzled as they started climbing down the rungs. "But you'll come with us, won't you?"

136

"We'll, er, follow you into space in our own ship," Teggs said. "You see, there's somewhere in particular we have to get to . . ."

"A long, long way from here," said Gipsy.

"Well, good luck." Zac shook hands and feet with all the astrosaurs as he followed them outside. He took a last look around at the scorched valley and the mountains as a clutch of colossal, clunky rocket-ships tore across the sky like deep red scratches in the blue.

"There goes Rokol and his carnivores," said Iggy. The rockets soon faded from sight. But the orange dot of the meteor burned ever more brightly.

137

"Time we were gone." Zac looked round at the other enormous tug-ships, two on either side of his own. He held up a big green flag to them, and the pilots waved green flags back at him. "With just an hour to spare, we're ready to go . . ." He climbed back up the ladder and waved to the astrosaurs. "So long!"

"So long *ago*," breathed Teggs as Zac got back into his tug-ship's control room. "And yet here we are, ready for—"

"BLAST OFF!" Zac hollered, and his tug-ship's engines fired into life with an incredible roar. The astrosaurs clung together as the ground began to shake. The four remaining tug-ships started up their mighty motors. Finally the *Soar-a-saurus*'s engines ignited with a rumbling thunderclap that seemed loud enough to shatter mountains.

Awestruck, Teggs watched the fierce blue flames gusting from the tug-ships' several jets, as each of them took

to the air. Their towropes, tied to the
sides of the *Soar-a-saurus*, grew taut and
tightened as they strained to help lift the
ark-ship's titanic weight. Teggs whooped
with delight as the *Soar-a-saurus*'s engines
roared even louder and thick, dungy
exhaust smoke swirled all around, while
the giant jets' flames turned incandescent
white. Then, finally, the humongous craft
rose into the sky, the tug-ships taking
her higher and
higher ...

"Have a good trip!" Gipsy hooted at top volume, and Iggy waved as the unlikely spaceships slowly dwindled from view into the upper atmosphere.

"That was amazing," said Teggs. "To think we saw such a historic moment with our own eyes."

Arx nodded, eyeing the meteor in the

sky. "But now it's time we were gone too."

"How true!" came a horrid hiss from behind them.

With a sinking feeling, Teggs turned to find that a familiar black-and-orange figure with an eye-patch had sneaked up in the storm of noise, smoke and dirt.

It was General Loki, a glint of evil relish in his only eye – and an atom gun clutched in his claws!

## Chapter Eleven

# A TRICK IN TIME

"You thought you could thwart my plans, didn't you?" rasped Loki. "Well, you were wrong!"

"We *have* thwarted them." Teggs squared up to the black-clad raptor.

"You might just have noticed the *Soar-a-saurus* has taken off – with thousands of plant-eaters safely aboard."

Loki chuckled. "Aboard perhaps, but not safely."

"What do you mean?" asked Arx.

"You checked those plants for poison," said Loki. "But you should have tested the *soil* in which they grew. Then you might've found the twelve bombs I'd hidden inside random pots!"

Gipsy and Iggy gasped, and Teggs stared in horror. "Bombs?"

"Magnificent micro-bombs!" Loki nodded gloatingly. "Super-explosive gunpowder sealed in a mega-metal shell. Completely tamper-proof! Once set, they cannot be defused."

Teggs scowled. "So Rokol *was* tricking us."

"No! The soft fool really did wish to suck up to you sap-sucking stinkheads." Loki spat on the ground. "He threw me

out of his camp –
I had to sneak
back inside
and plant
my bombs in
those baskets
when no one
was looking!"

"How long
before the explosives
go off?" Iggy demanded.

"They are set to detonate just
as the meteor strikes the Earth." Loki
sniggered. "The puny plant-eaters will
perish at the same time as their planet!"

Gipsy looked pale. "Captain, that
awful future we found at the other end
of the space tunnel, where meat-guzzling
dinos ruled the Earth and Mars and
everywhere else, and plant-eaters don't
exist . . . It's all going to happen, isn't it?"

"You've *seen* this future?" Loki's eyes
widened, and he cackled with delight.

"There you are, then – proof, astrosaurs, of your ultimate defeat!"

"No," said Teggs. "That was how the future was *before* we travelled back here to stop you. Now we're a part of history ourselves, we can put events back on track."

Loki waved his gun. "While I've got this? I don't think so."

"You haven't used it yet," Teggs observed coolly. "Which means you must want something from us."

"Correct." Loki narrowed his single eye. "When you stole my ship you threw out three mega-metal crates. One of those crates contained food, one contained spare parts for my death-flyer ... and the last contained my exo-suit."

Teggs's eyes widened. "And without that, you can't escape in your stolen time machine, can you?"

"But I must!" cried Loki. "First I shall make sure Rokol and his fleeing carnivores know it was I who killed all the plant-eaters, so that I'll become a legend throughout the universe. Then, when I return to my own time, I shall be a dinosaur god, worshipped by all! I'll have power over everyone and everything! So – hand over my exo-suit at once."

"But . . . we don't have it!" Gipsy protested.

Teggs nodded. "We used that crate to cushion our fall – but we didn't see your exo-suit inside."

"Captain!" Iggy gasped. "I've just realized – Zac told his helpers to gather up all the spare parts they could find in case they were useful in the future."

"But these parts are *from* the future," said Arx. "If dinosaurs today discover the secrets of technology that won't be invented until sixty-five million years from now . . ."

"It could change history as surely as those bombs will," said Teggs gravely. "We've got to get up to the *Soar-a-saurus* and sort things out!"

"Bah. So sickeningly noble as ever." Loki raised his gun. "All I care about is getting hold of an exo-suit. Give me yours, Teggs – or I'll shoot your friends."

"All right . . ." said Teggs slowly. "I'll fetch it."

"No tricks," Loki warned. "Or the stripy girl gets it first!"

Gipsy, Arx and Iggy watched helplessly as Teggs trudged over to the *Sauropod*'s shuttle, went inside and shut the door. Loki chuckled nastily.

"What are you laughing at?" came a familiar voice behind them.

Everyone spun round . . . to find Teggs was somehow behind them, and wearing his exo-suit! He punched Loki in the snout, and the raptor general went down like a sack of potatoes.

"Captain!"
squealed Gipsy
in delight.

Iggy was
baffled. "But
we saw you get
on board the
shuttle. How can
you be in two places at once?"

"The same way he could be in two
places at once back at the space prison,"
said Arx, smiling. "When he went to the
shuttle he must've put on his exo-suit and
used the time machine to send himself
five minutes back into the past!"

"Exactly!" Teggs agreed.

"But the pyramid blew a fuse when it
brought us here," Gipsy remembered.

"I tried pressing the blue demonstration
button as Zindi did," Teggs told her.
"There must have been just enough
power left to send myself back to when
the *Soar-a-saurus* was taking off. While

we were busy watching it and Loki was creeping up . . ."

"*You* crept up behind us all!" Gipsy realized.

"And I've been hiding behind that rock ever since," Teggs revealed, "just waiting to make a surprise reappearance and come to our rescue!"

Arx looked forlorn. "If only I'd fixed the time machine right away, we could travel back to this morning when Loki was planting his bombs and stop him!"

"Can't you do it now?" Iggy asked him.

"It might take hours and hours." Arx shook his head. "Always assuming I can do it at all!"

"Then we'll have to do things the hard way," Teggs said gravely. "Come on, let's drag Loki onto our shuttle and get after the *Soar-a-saurus*. The meteor's going to hit within the hour."

"And when it does," said Arx, "those bombs on board will explode. If we can't find them and defuse them in time, the plant-eaters will die, and Loki's twisted future will become reality."

Teggs nodded. "That's why we've got to succeed – we've just *got* to!"

Minutes later the astrosaurs were taking off in Shuttle Alpha. Loki lay sprawled in a heap at Teggs's feet, and did not stir as the small ship blasted away from the planet in a whirlwind of fire and dung-flavoured smoke.

"Step on it, Iggy," Teggs urged his friend as the shuttle soared up and away and the sky turned to space around them.

"If only communicators existed in this time!" Gipsy lamented. "We've got no way to warn Gazell and Zac of the danger they're in."

"Look! There's the *Soar-a-saurus*, up ahead." Arx pointed through the windscreen to where the enormous ramshackle ship was speeding through space; the tug-ships had done their job and were now fixed to its sprawling sides just as Zac had described. "And there's the meteor!"

Teggs swallowed hard. The meteor was close enough now to be clearly visible – a jagged rock miles across, tumbling out of the void on its deadly collision course with the Earth. "Head straight for the *Soar-a-saurus*, Ig."

"But there's nowhere to dock!" Iggy protested. "We can't get on board."

Teggs was already changing into his spacesuit. "I'll just have to spacewalk across to the cargo hold and use Loki's gun to blow a hole in the door. Everything's strapped down in there, so it shouldn't fall out into space."

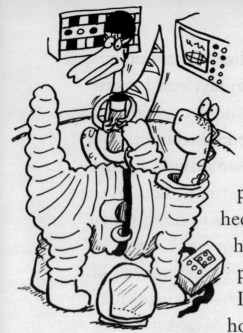

"You can use this sealing foam to block up the hole once you're inside." Gipsy passed Teggs a heavy spray can and he pushed it into his pocket. "Just like Iggy blocked the hole that Zac's tug-ship made in this shuttle."

"And since Loki hid the bombs in those baskets, he'll be the best one to find them." Teggs hauled the unconscious Loki to his feet and started stuffing him into another spacesuit. "Once he knows he'll be blown up along with his victims when the meteor hits Earth, I think he'll be willing to help."

Iggy steered alongside the *Soar-a-saurus*. Keeping tight hold of the general, Teggs took a long white rope that was attached to a metal platform at the back of the shuttle and clipped it to his suit. "Space ejector ready?"

"Ready," Iggy confirmed.

Teggs stood on the platform with Loki and took a deep breath. He had reached the final, desperate stage of the most vital mission of his life ...

"Send me out there, Ig," Teggs said. "Now!"

## Chapter Twelve

# DISASTER IN SPACE

Teggs gasped as the space ejector platform
shot upwards on a big pole. At the same
moment, a hatch in the ceiling slid open,
and he and Loki were pushed out into
starry darkness. The platform filled the
hatch-space so perfectly that not a breath
of air escaped from the shuttle. Teggs felt
a thrill of fear – had it not been for the
rope tethering his space suit to the shuttle

roof, he and Loki would be left drifting helplessly through the cosmos.

*And the plant-eater population would perish with us,* he thought.

Like a determined diver, Teggs used the shuttle roof as a springboard and launched himself towards the *Soar-a-saurus*'s cargo hold. He held Loki's wrist in one hand and the atom gun in the other.

But suddenly the tricky raptor twisted in his grip – and snatched the gun away!

*Loki was only* pretending *to be asleep,* Teggs realized. He tried to grab back the gun, but Loki kicked him in the belly and sent him crashing into the side of the *Soar-a-saurus.* Then, with an evil grin, the raptor put his gun to the space-rope and fired right through it.

Teggs's worst nightmare had come true – he was floating helplessly in space! Desperately he scrabbled for a grip on the giant ship, and just caught hold of one of the cargo door handles. Clinging on, he saw Loki's drooling jaws twist wide in a grin as he prepared to fire . . .

Back on the shuttle, Arx, Iggy and Gipsy watched the drama unfold in horror.

"Poor Teggs!" cried Gipsy. "He's done for!"

But then, with his free hand, Teggs grabbed the sealant spray and fired it at Loki's space helmet – SPLAT! Thick white foam covered the raptor's faceplate, and left him blinded.

Gipsy, Arx and Iggy cheered – but then Loki started firing wildly. One blast almost hit Teggs in the leg, another narrowly missed his back.

"Hang on, you two." Iggy twisted hard on the shuttle's flight stick. "I'm going to spoil Loki's aim!"

Gipsy and Arx gasped as their ship began to roll in a dizzying spin.

Dangling from the rope like a conker on the end of a string, Loki was swung round and round the shuttle. But still he was firing wildly.

"Nice job, Ig," said Gipsy as an atom-blast zipped past the windscreen. "But if he hits us, we haven't got any more sealing foam to keep in the air!"

Iggy groaned. "How can we get the captain back inside?"

Arx watched as the massive meteor rolled ever nearer. "And how can we get Loki's bombs out of the *Soar-a-saurus*?"

"If only there was more metal on the captain's spacesuit," said Gipsy, "we could use our space magnets to pull him back!"

Iggy shook his head. "We'd pull the *Soar-a-saurus* towards us too. It would crash into the shuttle . . ."

Suddenly Arx jumped into the air.

"Maybe not!" he cried, turning to the main controls and jabbing them with his horns. "If I can only change the settings in time . . ."

Gipsy stared. "What do you mean? What are you doing?"

"Trying to solve all our problems at once!" Arx yanked a wire from one circuit and plugged it into another. "Keep everything crossed, you two. We're going to need all the luck we can get!"

ZZAP! Dodging another of Loki's laser beams, Teggs banged with all his strength on the cargo hold's door. If only someone would let him inside – before it was too late. Already he could feel his grip on the

161

handle begin to slip. If he
let go now, he'd be lost
in space for ever . . .

Suddenly
something smashed
against the doors of
the cargo hold – from the
inside. CLANG! CLANG!! *CLANG!!!*
A series of little impacts sent vibrations
through the metal. And behind Loki,
Shuttle Alpha was starting to shake.
Teggs saw that its space magnets were
fully extended and shining an eerie blue.
He frowned. *Normally they glow red. What's
going on?*

Then the cargo doors were smashed
wide open by one of Loki's crates,
which had come whizzing
out from
inside.

Teggs clung to the handle as a dozen gleaming metal spheres swiftly followed it out into space like big bullets in a cloud of frozen soil.

"The bombs!" he breathed. "Somehow they've been sucked out of the *Soar-a-saurus*!"

Hope swelled inside Teggs's chest and gave him new strength to hold on. He watched in amazement as the shuttle switched off its magnets and shot upwards to avoid the deadly shower of bombs. Loki too was jerked up in the air like a puppet on a string as the projectiles hurtled past. Then the shuttle dropped back down again into position alongside the *Soar-a-saurus* and its magnets switched on again, shaking with power.

"Of course!" Teggs cried, his heart pounding. "Arx must've changed the magnets' settings so they only attract *mega*-metal!"

Still holding onto the space-rope, Loki finally clawed the foam from his helmet. "Curse you, astrosaurs!" he screamed, his one eye bright and narrowed with rage. "Curse you all, throughout eternity!"

"If I were you, Loki, I'd spend less time cursing and more time getting ready to dodge," Teggs cried. "If I'm right about our magnets attracting mega-metal — and if I've counted correctly — there are still two crates packed away on board the *Soar-a-saurus*. Any minute now you should be able to see for yourself . . ."

Right on cue, both big metal crates came rocketing out from inside the cargo hold. Loki had time for just a single squawk of outrage – then dropped both his gun and the rope as the biggest crate slammed into him. Again, Shuttle Alpha turned off its magnets and steered aside before Loki and his cube of mega-metal could crash into it. Instead, the crate's momentum carried the evil raptor out through space . . .

And straight into the path of the oncoming meteor!

SPLAMMMM! Teggs winced, his insides twisting in shock as the colossal rock roared past, snatching Loki, the crate and everything inside it from sight.

"Pulverized," Teggs muttered in shock. "My oldest enemy . . . gone for ever."

It was a terrible end to a terrible life, he decided.

But somehow, it seemed a fitting one.

# Chapter Thirteen

## GETTING BACK

Teggs was still dangling helplessly when
two big, quilted, spiky somethings dropped
down in front of his face.

They were
stegosaurus tails –
in spacesuits!

Gratefully, Teggs
let go of the cargo
door handle and
held onto the tails
as Zac and Gazell
heaved him inside.
Amid scattered
plants and baskets, Teggs
could see them both – and Gazell's little

hatchlings – all wearing space helmets and looking down at him with concern.

"Teggs!" said Zac. "I thought you weren't coming with us?"

"We heard all the banging," said Gazell. "What's been going on? It looks like a bomb went off in here!"

Teggs gave her a crooked smile. "You're closer than you know." He pointed to where the Earth's disc was slowly dwindling in the distance. "What's about to happen there will tell us if we're safe or—"

Even as he spoke, a pinprick of light flared on the surface of the planet: the nameless meteor had struck. Teggs watched, transfixed, as a dark cloud billowed up from the fiery spot and began to blanket the Earth.

"The end," he murmured. "And a new beginning."

Then twelve fierce explosions bloomed in nearby space as Loki's bombs went off – harmlessly. The hatchlings oohed and ahhed at the storm of fire and light, staring in wonder.

"Whoa!" Zac shielded his eyes. "What was that?"

"That," said Teggs, "was the end of poor old loopy Loki's final evil scheme to wipe you out. Thanks to my amazing crew, it failed."

Zac blinked, bewildered. Then he grinned and shook Teggs by the hand. "You four have done so much to help us. We shall sing your praises every day, all across space, so you will never be forgotten."

"Er, actually –" Teggs smiled ruefully – "it's probably a good idea if you keep very, very quiet about us. I can't explain, but it's for the best."

"Well," said Gazell, "there's one thing I can do to remember you." She scooped her youngest hatchling from her back and held him up to Teggs. "I've finally decided what to call this little tyke! I shall name him after *you*."

"Wow! Cool!" Teggs blushed. "So he'll be Teggs, er . . . I'm sorry, Gazell, I don't know your second name . . ."

"I'd like it to be 'Stegosaur'," Zac blurted. "Gazell – will you marry me?"

Gazell stared at him in shock. Then she hugged him tight and her hatchling jumped on him too. "Yes! Yes, I will!"

Teggs gulped. *So there he is*, he thought. *Teggs Stegosaur the first!*

Could it be possible? Was he looking at his own distant ancestor – his great-great-great-times-a-million-billion-great-grandfather?

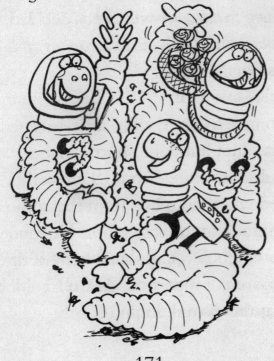

A little dizzily, Teggs turned to the *Sauropod* shuttle flying alongside, and saw Iggy, Arx and Gipsy waving through the windows. He saluted them, and then waved back happily.

*It's hard to know for sure,* Teggs decided. *But right now, I think the future for us all is looking very bright indeed!*

A few minutes later, with super-precise steering, Iggy brought Shuttle Alpha right alongside the *Soar-a-saurus* so that Teggs could simply hop from the cargo hold onto the little ship's roof! He landed on the hatch cover, grabbed hold of the remains of the rope, and took a final look back at the distant, raging Earth.

Then the ejector platform sucked him back inside – and into the waiting arms of his happy friends.

"Captain!" Arx cried. "Thank space you're back safely."

Teggs grinned. "Thank space *you* rejigged the magnets to work only on mega-metal."

Arx looked pleased. "Oh, it was nothing really."

"I don't think Loki would thank you," Iggy declared. "So it's just as well there's nothing really left of him – or his death-flyer, that time machine or any other technology, now that the meteor's trashed it all."

"But will there be anything left of our future?" said Gipsy nervously. "Has our being here in the past helped history stay on track – or wrecked it?"

"If Arx can only fix the time machine, we'll find out," said Teggs, already stripping off his quilted space gear. "By travelling forward sixty-five million, one hundred thousand and fifty-six years to the present – where this all began!"

Teggs thought he might go crazy, cooped up in the little shuttle for hours and hours, wondering if they would be trapped in the past for ever. But although it took Arx the better part of a day, he was able to repair the golden pyramid in the end. The astrosaurs put on their exo-suits and prepared for the first leg of their long journey back home.

Arx nudged the time machine's on-button with his nose-horn. "Here goes everything," he murmured as the metal pyramid hummed into life.

At once, Teggs felt the shuttle begin to shudder and shake. The familiar flash of red light sparked through his head. He was spinning, spiralling, lost . . .

Then, with a gigantic lurch, the shuttle stopped shaking and all was still. Teggs let out a sigh of relief and opened his eyes.

"I think we're back in our own time, Captain," Arx said breathlessly, studying the time machine's readout.

Iggy checked the shuttle controls. "We're back where we started, between Earth and Mars."

"It all seems quiet," said Gipsy, staring out into space. "But did we win, or . . . ?"

She left the question hanging.

"*Sauropod*," said Teggs, speaking urgently into the communicator. "This is your captain in Shuttle Alpha. Can you hear me?"

Only whispers of static could be heard through the speakers.

Teggs tried again. "Come in, *Sauropod*, please?" He swallowed hard. "Anyone?"

Then a loud chirp came through loud and clear.

Gipsy cheered. "It's Sprite!"

A babble of chirps crackled from the communicator, and Gipsy quickly translated for Iggy's benefit: *"Captain, I don't know what happened. One minute those crazy carnivore ships were shooting us with everything they had, the next they—"*

"Vanished?" Teggs interrupted.

Sprite made squawks and clicking noises. *"Yes!"* Gipsy continued. *"The bad carnivores just faded away. It was as if . . . they'd never existed."*

"That's because they never *did* exist."

Arx was grinning as he stared through his astro-scope. "Look at the Earth! Just look at it!"

Teggs, Iggy and Gipsy quickly crowded round to see. There were no giant snarling reptiles all over the place. The planet was plastered with billions of human beings.

Gipsy whooped. "The Earth's back to normal!"

"If you can call those funny-looking humans normal!" said Iggy.

"Right now, I call them the most welcome sight in the universe," said Teggs. "All this proves that we haven't harmed history after all – we've simply given it a helping hand. So let's catch up with the *Sauropod* and travel back through the space tunnel. I'm glad we visited Earth, but now I'm ready to stay in the real home of the dinosaurs."

"The Jurassic Quadrant," said Gipsy dreamily. "I can't wait!"

## Chapter Fourteen

## PRESENT IN THE PRESENT!

Although shaken and battered – much like her crew – the *Sauropod* held together stoutly on the bone-jarring, mind-squashing return voyage through the space tunnel. And when the astrosaurs arrived at DSS HQ, they were informed that Admiral Rosso was waiting for them in the cavernously grand Extra-Special Suite for Very Important Dinosaurs.

As Teggs led his tired, terrific team through the suite's marble doors, he saw that Rosso wasn't alone. A whole crowd of dinos were gathered there with party poppers.

"SURPRISE!" came the huge shout

from all assembled, as the poppers went
off and streamers flew. The dimorphodon
launched joyfully into the air, catching
the streamers and twirling them about
like banners.

"You and your crew have done the plant-eater race proud this day, Teggs," Rosso declared. "And so I thought you deserved a small reward – the biggest, poshest party in dinosaur history!"

Iggy grinned. "We know a lot about history, sir!"

"So, party on, dudes!" A stocky green diplodocus stepped out from behind the admiral, with a yellow pterosaur perched on his back.

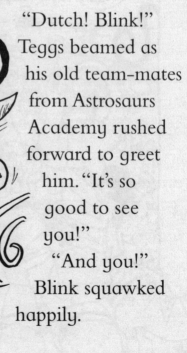

"Dutch! Blink!" Teggs beamed as his old team-mates from Astrosaurs Academy rushed forward to greet him. "It's so good to see you!"

"And you!" Blink squawked happily.

"And wherever the Daring Dinos go, can Damona's Darlings be far away?" A pretty red diceratops stepped forward to join them. "Hi, everyone!"

"Damona!" Teggs cried. "My old Academy rival, how are you?"

"Brilliant, of course!" Damona fluttered her eyelids. "As are *my* old team-mates, Splatt and Netta . . ."

"Wow," said Teggs as Netta the pink ankylosaur gave him a hug and Splatt the dryosaurus shook his hand. "The old gang really is all here."

"Along with some newer faces too," said Governor Bunwinkle, their friend from the space prison. "Well done, astrosaurs."

"Yes, and thank you," said Zindi Bent beside him, free of chains now. "Thank you for stopping Loki using my machine to destroy history."

Rosso smiled down at her. "Zindi is being released at once with a full pardon," he revealed. "She will join our top inventors' team at Super-Secure-Space-Station One, using her amazing mind to build many more marvellous machines that will help sea-reptiles and plant-eaters alike."

"I'm pleased to hear it," said Teggs.

Zindi grinned. "Well, you've certainly proved to me that my time machine is way too dangerous to stay in existence."

"Indeed it is," Rosso agreed. "Tomorrow, we'll take it to pieces. But right now, all of you

– enjoy the party! I've laid on the biggest buffet in the galaxy . . ."

"Laid on it? I hope you didn't squash it, dude," joked Dutch.

"Eeep," agreed Sprite as two dozen dimorphodon fell about with laughter.

"It's the way he tells them," said Netta dryly.

But Teggs hardly heard them. His eyes were out on stalks at the sight of the super-big table at the back of the room, weighed down with about a thousand plates of succulent-looking plants – including one that looked very familiar. "That's never a bowl of garga-weeds is it?"

"Newly discovered by the Supply Fleet on a distant planet," said Splatt proudly.

"That's a blast from the past I'm happy to see!"

Hunger and happiness filling his whole body, Teggs ran over and started tucking in greedily. "Delicious!"

Arx, Iggy and Gipsy ran over to join him in filling their plates.

"It's hard to believe that Zac and Gazell lived so many millions of years ago," said Gipsy. "I wish we could visit them a few years later to see how they got on . . ."

"Too dangerous," Arx declared.

"I'm sure they took good care of each other," said Iggy. "And of their family."

*Including the very first little Teggs Stegosaur,*
thought Teggs happily.

He looked around the room again
and saw other old friends in the crowd.
There was Shazz, the High Flapper
from Squawk Major, talking to Sprite
and the dimorphodon . . . Prime
Rhino Serras from the sunny world of
Hawn was chatting to Jodril, the big-
eyed apatosaurus . . . Queen Soapi the
bactrosaur was fanning herself weakly
while Leefer, the astrosaurs' smelly farmer

friend from Noxia-4, told her tales about his life . . . Spink, a friendly kentrosaurus miner, was chatting with Hank and Crank, star athletes of the Great Dinosaur Games . . .

Teggs wandered around the room, talking and laughing with them all for hours. He was glad to see his crew having fun too. Arx was delighted when his niece Abbiz burst in and came rushing up to hug him, just as Iggy was thrilled to find his brother Wimvis on the scene with two frothing flagons of top-quality fern-juice.

Gipsy broke off from a chinwag with Netta and Damona and tapped Teggs on the shoulder. "You looked miles away, Captain. A penny for your thoughts?"

"I was just thinking – who needs a time machine?" said Teggs. "With good friends and memories, we can relive past escapades whenever we like – and look forward to new adventures still to come."

"I'll drink to that," said Iggy, raising his cup.

"So will I!" chorused Arx and Gipsy.

"And I'll drink to *us*," said Teggs, grinning at his fantastic friends. "Here's to the astrosaurs – and to a frantic, fun-filled future for us all!"

# ASTRO PUZZLE TIME

## EARTH ATTACK!
## QUIZ Questions

1. What does DSS stand for?

2. What did Zindi Bent invent?

3. What is an exo-suit and what does it do?

4. How did Loki and the Astrosaurs reach Earth so quickly?

5. What did Gipsy and Teggs do to disguise themselves when they reached carnivore camp?

6. What flavour coffee did Gipsy drink in the DSS canteen?

## Answers:

1. Dinosaur Space Service

2. She invented a time machine

3. Part-costume, part-machine, it allows the wearer to travel through time safely

4. They went through a space tunnel

5. They used sharp stones for fangs and Teggs disguised his backplates with mud

6. Fern Coffee

# ASTRO PUZZLE TIME

All this time travel has made things change a little. Can you spot the five differences between these images?

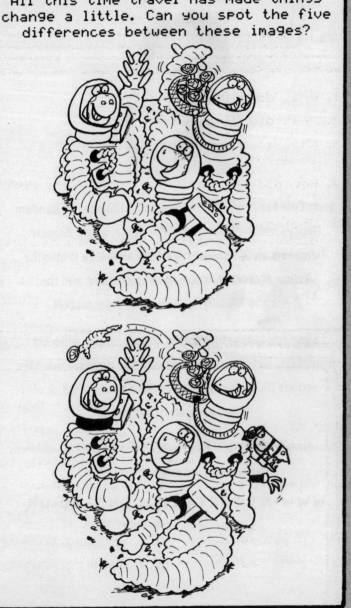

# ABOUT THE AUTHOR

Photo: RebeccaJudge.com

Steve Cole has now written fifty books published by Random House Children's Books. As well as the hugely popular *Astrosaurs* and *Astrosaurs Academy* series, he is also the author of *Cows in Action* and *Slime Squad*, and the *Z. Rex* and *Tripwire* sequences for older readers.

Steve has also written lots of other books for different publishers, including several *Doctor Who* novels which have become UK bestsellers. He has also been the editor of fiction and non-fiction titles.

Steve lives in Buckinghamshire with his wife and two children. You can find out more about him at

**www.stevecolebooks.co.uk**

Visit WWW.**stevecolebooks**.CO.UK for
fun, games, jokes, to meet the characters
and much, much more!

Welcome to a world where dinosaurs fly
spaceships and cows use a time-machine...

Sign up for the free Steve Cole monthly
newsletter to find out what your favourite
author is up to!

**There are lots more Steve Cole books for you to try. Take a peek at some of these . . .**

# Meet the time-travelling cows!

# THE TER-MOO-NATORS

## BY STEVE COLE

IT'S 'UDDER' MADNESS!

Genius cow Professor McMoo and his trusty
sidekicks, Pat and Bo, are the star agents of the
C.I.A. –short for COWS IN ACTION! They travel
through time, fighting evil bulls from the future and
keeping history on the right track . . .

When Professor McMoo invents a brilliant TIME
MACHINE, he and his friends are soon attacked by
a terrifying TER-MOO-NATOR – a deadly robo-cow
who wants to mess with the past and change the
future! And that's only the start of an incredible
ADVENTURE that takes McMoo, Pat and Bo from a
cow paradise in the future to the SCARY dungeons
of King Henry VIII . . .

It's time for action. **COWS IN ACTION.**

# READ ALL THE

## COWS IN ACTION

## ADVENTURES!

COMING
SOON!

# IF YOU CAN'T TAKE THE SLIME – DON'T DO THE CRIME!

## THE SLIME SQUAD VS THE FEARSOME FISTS

### BY STEVE COLE

Plog, Furp, Zill and Danjo aren't just monsters in a rubbish dump. Together they are the **SLIME SQUAD** – crime-busting super-monsters, here to save their whiffy world!

Trashland is in trouble. Fierce and fearsome fist-creatures are on the rampage, robbing banks and causing panic. Only four brave and slightly slimy monsters can possibly stop them . . . Are they up to the challenge? Or will the Fists flatten them and rule over all with an iron hand . . ?